SOUTHERN STYLE

Short Stories and Recipes from a Southern Foodie

SOUTHERN STYLE

Short Stories and Recipes from a Southern Foodie

by Brett Prince

Copyright © 2024

Brett Prince

Paperback ISBN: 978-1-964818-98-6

All Rights Reserved. Any unauthorized reprint or use of this material is strictly prohibited. No part of this book may be reproduced or transmitted in any form or by any means, electronic or mechanical, including photocopying, recording, or by any information storage and retrieval system without express written permission from the author.

All reasonable attempts have been made to verify the accuracy of the information provided in this publication. Nevertheless, the author assumes no responsibility for any errors and/or omissions.

DEDICATION

This book is for the many people who still hold dear the art of cooking food. It is a tip of the hat to the students of Culinary Arts who have devoted their lives to the wonderful world of preparing food. It is holding a door for the mother with the baby in her arms and the shopping cart full of groceries, which, even with her busy schedule at home and work, still cooks at least one meal a day and ensures that her family gathers around the dinner table to eat. To the elderly women and men out there who reflect on days passed when they actually had a dinner bell that Momma would ring when it was time for them to come in and eat, this hopefully will bring back those wonderful memories. To my home state of Mississippi and to the growers, the preparers, and the consumers of food, this is my love letter to all of you.

Table of Contents

Genesis i

Introduction What is Southern Style? iii

Chapter 1 A Child of Nature: 1

Chapter 2 The Grandparents: 37

Chapter 3 What on God's Green Earth? 61

Chapter 4 Supper Time: 102

Chapter 5 The Gulf Coast: 127

Chapter 6 Jazzin' It Up: 149

Chapter 7 The Good Ol' Boys: 189

Chapter 8 Icing on the Cake: 198

Genesis

The sun has just started sinking behind the trees across the river. The current hums its low, pulsating bass line, and the crickets and frogs have now formed their ensemble. In the distance comes the deep percussion of a towboat's engines thumping. A few minutes pass, and she rounds the bend to make her grand appearance. I think back to another time when the great steamboats ran this river and, for a second, feel like Huck Finn, about to slide his raft into the turbulent waters, going to meet ol' Tom Sawyer to share a pipe and discuss today's mischief.

The river does this from time to time; it grabs one's imagination and totally displaces them from the modern world. Artists have tried for centuries to capture her magnificent beauty but to no avail. There are thousands of paintings of picturesque sunsets and stern-wheel vessels navigating her tricky channels, but for a person to gain a true sense of this majestic body of water, they have to stand on those muddy banks just watching and listening. The natural world, still as it is, cannot be captured in a frozen frame.

While the music plays in three-quarter time, the water delivers scents of jasmine, honeysuckle, and the egregious hint of fertilizer from upstream. Amidst eddies and whirlpools, driftwood twirls and dances like ballerinas to the rhythm of the Waltz of God's Creation. This perfectly choreographed play, tethered directly to His hand, continues on without rest, even once the sun has been replaced by the moon and the lightning bugs take center stage.

As the Mighty Mississippi charms her way through locks and lofty bluffs, down through the flatlands, and eventually to her slumber in the shining Gulf, her waters are tinged with hickory smoke, casino lights, crawfish boils, blues, and zydeco music. This cultural cocktail is the preferred drink of the beautiful sirens of the deep, who call out to everyone in their angelic voices, begging them to please come south.

Come and taste the spices of Creole food, the sweet, oak-aged bourbon of Kentucky, the wild blackberries of Mississippi, and the succulent barbecue of western Tennessee. Hear the gritty guitars of the Delta blues and the brassy jazz of New Orleans. Wander through the cavernous hills of Arkansas. Take a stroll along the sandy beaches of the Gulf Coast, with its squatting live oak arms spread wide, inviting you to stay forever.

Introduction
What is Southern Style?

"Southern Style" is a phrase that folks who usually aren't from the South use to describe food that, in their minds, represents something that Southerners eat. Well, bless their little hearts for thinking that by adding bacon or buttermilk to some generic recipe, it could then be compared to real Southern food. It ain't that simple. If you are not in the South, then you cannot cook Southern food; no more than I can sit at my house and cook Hawaiian food. I don't have access to the local ingredients. With a few skills and knowledge of the culture, we can recreate something that mimics the cuisine, but it would still be nothing more than a rumor without the right ingredients. The crisis we face is that Southerners aren't cooking Southern food these days; they are following "Southern Style" recipes that have led them away from cooking Southern food the way that it was intended.

I cannot for the life of me see the reason why anyone would go through the act of writing recipes in intricate detail without telling the story of the food with the same passion. If all that is left to be of my beloved Southern cuisine is a compilation of orders and decrees for how to prepare a dish, then we, as Southerners, should consider a renouncement of cooking, take all future meals from a box, and move on to lead more meaningful lives; we have failed as a culture. Every food has a story, just like every person, and we are stock of the greatest storytellers this world has ever seen. So why do we surrender a skill that, for so long, has defined us? It is sheer ecstasy for me to sit in the company of the great storytellers, and I would not be who I am today without them. Since the day that I was delivered into the cosmos, I have had an intense desire to be around other people. I love people with graceful manners, who speak the language of romance and validation, and those whose conversations ebb and flow like the moon-driven tides of the continental rims. I am mesmerized by people with great skills. Watching someone swiftly chop an onion with a chef's knife is like staring into a fire. So, let's have a long talk about my part of the world. Hop in the truck, and let me take you for a ride through the country.

Before we hit the road, there is something that I want to be honest about. I didn't set out to write a book that had stories in it. My idea was to expose all of my family's recipes in a basic format that resembled a cookbook created by a robot that was made in China. About a quarter of the way through, I felt like I was finally, after 38 years of living on this planet, following the well-beaten path. I've tried that before, and that's where I always got lost. I've never been able to see things in black and white; I see them in forest green, ocean blue, and red dirt. The people who helped raise me didn't just teach me to "smell the roses"; they taught me to see the beauty in them, to know each one of them by name, and to be in love with the colors they offer to the world.

I love to cook for people, and what I love most about doing so is the little spaces in between the prepping, cooking, and eating stages; I mostly love the conversations. So, the idea of simply writing a cookbook chock full of recipes didn't make the cut; it needed something more. I figured that if I was going to give you the steps to preparing the dish, it would be incomplete without also giving you the backstories and origins of some of them. I do not claim to be anything more than a blue-collar, middle-class guy, and I have never taken a class, other than Basic English, that would help me write a book. What I do have is an eye for detail due to my upbringing as an avid outdoorsman and a passion for all things of the Divine Creation. I have tried my best to harness my wandering mind, but, to no one's surprise, the straps broke, and I just said to hell with it. Most of the stories I grew up listening to were muddied up, either in the mind of the listeners or out of the mouth of the one telling them, with many distractions such as whiskey, sweltering heat, or nagging mosquitoes. There are gaps in my mind of a lot of the events that have taken place in my life, voids that I cannot go back and unlock.

My past is a rocky one, a whirlwind of destruction and chaos. Like a lot of folks from my neck of the woods, I've been on every side of good and evil. The two angels on my shoulders do nothing but fight all the time, and up until I found myself in prison, I never really knew which one was my friend. I'm not proud of a lot of that past, but I'm also not ashamed. There are little nuggets of good all throughout this life that I tend to focus on. Rather than let feelings of remorse, despair, or shame be the barricades that block my path to anything good, I just keep moving. My mind's transmission has no reverse, only forward and neutral. I spend most of my time in neutral, just idling and waiting on the next sunrise, which will likely bring another challenge and another piece to this crazy jigsaw puzzle of life. I pray that I never find them all.

So fasten your seatbelt, sit back, and enjoy the ride. These roads are a little bumpy, and we may wind up in a mud hole or two. That's okay, though, because I drive a four-wheel drive. And roll that window up; you're letting the cold air out. I don't care what you saw the boys from Florida Georgia Line do in their music video; we don't ride with the windows down in the summer because it's too hot for that, plus it lets dust in. And those fancy lifted trucks, with the oversized wheels and low-profile tires that stick out of the fender wells a foot or more; we call them "Pavement Princesses," and we don't drive them. Those things are ridiculous and will get stuck on wet grass. Let's get past all the pandering and down into the heart and soul of Southern culture.

Driving along the old back roads that twist and turn like rivers, meandering nowhere in particular, gives me a deeper appreciation for the things that God has provided for us to enjoy in our time here on earth. Turning onto the broken asphalt and heading out of town is like entering a portal into a magical world of wildlife, gravel-bottomed creeks, and virgin forests. The journey through these enchanted lands sets my soul ablaze and stirs it like a pot of gumbo, releasing endorphins that can only be described with the most beautiful language there has ever been: English, in a backwoods, Southern dialect. Yes, it is indeed exhilarating and euphoric and intoxicating, but to a guy like me, well, it's simply something else.

See, I'm country. Sure, I know how to speak properly and present myself as a slightly sophisticated human being if I have to. I just designed my life so that I rarely have to. It isn't something that I enjoy doing, and I would rather spend that time in my own circle, among my kind of people, doing things that don't require us to be prim and proper. The people I speak of don't get all dressed up to go out on the town; they just wear jeans and boots. If you're lucky, they might change out of their work clothes and into a decent T-shirt. Most of us are educated in areas that a lot of people aren't. Most of those teachings, such as how to operate heavy machinery or sharpen a knife, came from our elders and were passed down as practical wisdom. Some of us chose a different form of education that allowed us to do things in life that don't require hard hats and steel-toe boots. None of us think that getting dirt on our hands is any kind of a big deal; we just wipe it on our jeans.

There is a theory among Southerners that if we let our children play in the dirt, it will build their immunity and help them fight off common illnesses. Being intrigued by this, as well as having a love for planting things in that same dirt, I became a student of soil chemistry and microbiology. I never really made soil-borne illnesses in children the main focal point of my studies. It confuses me because I have actually seen more than one child *eat* dirt, and a lot of times, they will do it when you aren't looking. So, having no control point to start from, I just gave up on figuring out if the dirt itself played a role in their health and well-being. My conclusion was that the microbes in the soil actually did improve the immune system by inhibiting the child's gut. The healthy bacteria fight against the bad ones and create a biome that functions as a fortress, guarding the child against the enemy. It is just a theory of mine to go along with what people down here already have reason to believe, but I decided to leave that up to the experts. Instead, I turned my studies towards agriculture. Over the years, I have learned a lot about the way plants live in certain environments. It has been a fun and wonderful journey, and some of it has been beyond my mind's ability to take in. I feel like I have come a long way, but I still have an even longer way to go. But I pity the ones who have chosen that same path without the vital knowledge that you obtain from tending a garden in a region with heavy clay soil, hundred-degree summers, a profusion of root-destroying nematodes, and plant diseases that are too many to list. If it were not for my parents and grandparents teaching me their unorthodox ways of gardening from the time I was a child, there would be no way for me to grasp the knowledge of this now. It would be like beginning a novel in the middle and trying to figure out the characters and the setting; possible but complicated. I also studied Culinary Arts, focusing intensely on French cooking methods, but without my Louisiana-born grandmother, I wouldn't know a damn thing about how to actually cook food.

I was raised by country folks, the kind of people who were so poor that shoes became family heirlooms. Out of pure necessity, they had to know how to build things, grow their own food, and cook and preserve that food without any failure, or they would do without. My daddy quit school in the eighth grade and went to work to help support the family because his daddy squandered what little money they did have on booze, prostitutes, and Seven-Card Stud. Like a lot of poor families in this world, they suffer in ways that the average person can't even imagine. To say they were dysfunctional would be a huge understatement.

When daddy was just a kid, his old man came home one night stumbling drunk, then he sprawled out across the kitchen table and started pulling wads of cash out of every pocket. Being more money than they had probably ever seen, my grandmother quickly devised a plan for how to keep it. She quietly walked the children out to their 1953 Chevrolet and told them all to get inside, and when she ran back out of the house to duck down to the floorboard and keep their heads down. She went back inside and a few minutes later came back out with both hands full of cash. When she got back to the car and jumped into the driver's seat, she had just closed the door when the first shot rang out. She slammed the car in reverse, and by the time they were out of sight, that old Chevy had six bullet holes down the left side. That was the father of seven children showing them what was truly important to him, I guess. He may have gotten lucky and won it fair and square playing poker, or he may have carved someone up with a knife and taken the money. Who really knows? But we do know that my grandmother robbed that old bastard blind and sped away like Bonnie and Clyde.

Daddy's older brother, my uncle Buddy, landed a great job running moonshine shortly after the family moved to Jackson in 1962. Buddy loved the old Ford cars, with their sleek bodies, beautiful interiors, and roaring engines. One night in 1963, he was working late and got himself into a high-speed chase coming back into town. Those cars didn't handle curves like the cars of today, and he rolled it over in a sharp corner, got arrested, and had to serve three months in jail. Upon his release, and with a little money he had saved up from work, he bought a very fine red and white 1956 Ford Crown Victoria. He welded ninety pounds of railroad iron along each side of the frame to lower the car's center of gravity so that it would handle better. Next time, he wouldn't get caught.

Maybe the cops were on to him, or maybe it was just coincidence, but it wasn't long before he found himself in another police chase. Everything was going smooth, and he had put some distance between himself and Johnny Law when he took a curve just a little too fast, and the car lost traction, with its overly tight suspension, and slid down an embankment and into the Ross Barnett Reservoir. He instantly killed the engine and headlights and watched from his sinking car as the cops drove right on by in pursuit of him.

Neither Uncle Buddy nor my father could swim. When I asked Daddy why they never learned how to, his response was that they never had time to learn. That sounds silly, but I believe it to be nothing short of the truth. Buddy managed to kick and flail his way to shore and escape his doom that day. That car is still on the bottom of the reservoir to this day with a trunk-load of white lightning. He died in the 1970s while fishing in the Pearl River off of Lakeland Drive, while his two sons, my cousins Chris and Andy, swam safely ashore. Chris and Andy are car guys, just like their daddy was.

My grandfather on my momma's side was much different from the other one. He was the type of man that dogs follow around, and children wanted to sit in his lap all the time. He was a family man and was faithful to them and *almost* everyone else in his life. This man was my moral compass, always redirecting me and teaching me how not to be a heathen. I don't want to spoil the fun, but most of his teachings didn't adhere. Because of the abundance of Scottish blood coursing through my veins, I always saw the gamblers and bootleggers as the heroes. It's said that good guys wear white hats and bad guys wear black hats. Well, I wear a cowboy hat a lot of times, and every single one I've ever worn was brown. So that may just be the sum of my existence. I am both and neither.

One year, we all went on vacation to Walt Disney World during the 2008 Spring Break season. Somewhere around Panama City, we passed a car full of young high school girls in a little sedan with the words "Honk If You're Horny" painted on the back window in white shoe polish. I was the lead car in the convoy, with almost my entire family behind me, all trying to follow different GPS routes and stopping every hundred miles, the way tourists do. I made it to the resort a good hour ahead of everyone else, with my grandmother and grandfather second in line. Everyone else pulled up shortly behind them and started unloading their vehicles for our week-long stay. My grandfather asked, "Did ya'll see them, girls?" I knew exactly which ones he was talking about: the ones we passed 250 miles back. I guess they were still on his mind. My grandmother said, "Johnnie, everyone saw those girls with 'honk if you're horny' painted on their window. Tell them what you did."

"I sat down on it."

The horn was what he was implying he "sat down" on. She said he blew it for two minutes straight. Now, this man was in his 70s at the time and still flirting with the high school girls spring breaking in Panama City, Florida. Brothers and sisters, to this day, I have never laughed harder than I did then.

This book is about truth. I am going to reveal many truths about not just myself and my family but food and Southern culture as well. I would be doing a disservice to us all if I sat here and told you that my grandfather on my momma's side was some kind of saint. By definition, he was a criminal. He was just the funny kind. Like a millionaire who robs candy stores, my grandfather committed crimes out of sheer pleasure. He used to work for the

Borden Milk Company as a delivery driver and would steal milk and trade it for beef with a friend of his who owned a meat market. Beef was very expensive in those days, but my momma says that they ate steak dinners every week when she was growing up, sometimes multiple times a week. He and my grandma used to go on vacations to places like Alaska and the Caribbean, and he would always bring me things back from these exotic places. One time, he smuggled ten Cuban cigars back in a large medicine bottle and gave them to me. I don't know why they are illegal, but they most definitely are. I could go on and on about his petty crimes, but since he has a clean record with the law, I declined to write his rap sheet. What my grandfather did was introduce me to the finer things in life, not through materialistic items with any monetary value but fragments of different cultures.

He would take us camping all the time, but not just sitting around campfires making smores; he made each trip an adventure. He would school us on the native plants, tell us what rivers named things like "Homochitto" by the Native Americans meant in our language (which is "Big Red," in case you were wondering), and carry us through passages of time with his elaborate and hilariously detailed stories. Once, he brought me a little wooden box from Alaska, and inside that box was smoked Sockeye salmon. He explained how the people set the traps in the rivers and how it took one week of preparing and cold-smoking the fish to create this marvelous dish.

At ten years old, I learned from him how to "set" the cream, then skim it and pour it into the churn, and the rhythm you have to keep during the process to effectively separate the butter and the buttermilk, how salting the butter makes it taste rancid, and that the buttermilk actually tastes good. And because of his theft and years of practice of grilling free prime Angus beef, I had the greatest instructor in the world to teach me how to cook a steak properly. So, I got to be a part of a culture that has little to do with social classes and economics but leans more towards traditions and food; lucky me.

So, to me, "Southern Style" isn't just a recipe or a cast-iron skillet that has been handed down through six generations. It isn't a jug of overly-sweetened iced tea and a fold-out lawn chair under the shade of a giant magnolia tree. It's not worn-out boots, blue tick hounds, your daddy's old pump-twelve, John Deere tractors, or even a little girl with two first names wearing a Sunday dress and eating a cold slice of watermelon with just a sprinkle of salt. It's every one of those things and more.

"Southern Style" is a front porch conversation with an old man who begins every story with an introduction of a year that you probably don't even know who the president was at the time. Oh, but he does. "Southern Style" is knowing to tap that chair a couple of times with the tip of your boot before you sit because it's been a while since anyone else has sat in it, and red wasps may have a nest on the bottom. "Southern Style" is when one stings you, having a pinch of snuff handy to pack on it and draw the poison out. "Southern Style" is purple-hull peas, collard greens, fried pork chops with pan gravy, and a slice of hot cornbread that was cooked by someone who constantly complains about the weather and will never figure out how to use a Smartphone. "Southern Style" is doing all of this out of instinct because, in our day-to-day lives, it's the norm.

Down here, things move slowly. Some call us Southerners old-fashioned and say we're behind in the times, which is quite fine by us. Modern times can be stressful, and we don't need any stress that poverty and high humidity haven't already offered. But regardless of the rest of the world's preconceived notions, there's no denying that we make some damn fine food. Why do you think the Yankees incessantly attempt to reproduce it? Why does such a backward place (as some believe it to be) have its own cuisine?

So many strange myths have evolved around Southern food, but, just like any attempt to degrade or destroy something great, the shot gets deflected. When I hear someone say that catfish are nasty fish because they are bottom feeders, two things instantly come to mind:

a) Catfish are not just bottom feeders and probably eat the same amount of their food off of the bottom as most any other fish.

b) Almost every living thing on this planet eats off of the ground.

So the bottom feeding point is moot, along with other manufactured health risks and suggestions like "Southern food is just too spicy." Put however much damn spice you want in it. Southerners aren't fire-breathing dragons, and our tongues are made the same as any other human being. This brings us back to the question of "What is Southern Style?" Is it simply the ingredients of a very simple and basic cuisine that is rooted primarily in Africa and France? Or could it be the appreciation for the food and the love that goes into the preparation of it? We'll get to the nuts and bolts of it, but first, let us pray.

"Heavenly Father, we thank You for the opportunity to come together and celebrate this life You have given us. We thank You for the most wonderful gift of all: Your Son, Christ Jesus. As we stumble along on our journey through this world, we ask that You continue to be our guiding light, shining Your brilliance upon the path to Your Kingdom. Teach us to be kind to one another and to never fear doing the right thing. We trust in You, oh Mighty God. Along with the blessings of forgiveness and love, You have invested in us the power to pass those blessings along to Your entire Creation. We have received Your Grace; help us now to grow stronger in our faith. In Your precious Son Jesus' name we pray."

Amen

Chapter 1
A Child of Nature:

Now, most authors of books are highly educated people, especially in the area of writing. This one is not. I am not a descendant of a family of Southern aristocrats, and school was not something I was very good at when I was growing up. The playground didn't have a pond stocked with catfish, and the teachers wouldn't allow kids to cuss or keep a pocketknife. It was hell on earth. I believe that there are really only two types of people in this world: academically inclined and mechanically inclined. Anyone who is a good combination of those two has spread themselves too thin and cannot be trusted. I have a good friend named Kyle who scored high enough on the A.C.T. to receive an academic scholarship to Baylor University. He has to be told when it's raining outside. I have known Kyle my whole life and would still never dream of loaning him a chainsaw.

I happen to be the mechanically inclined type. In the pitch black dark of night, I can back a boat trailer down a slippery ramp and, by pure instinct, know when I've gotten just enough of it in the water so that the boat floats off on the first attempt. I can reach my hand into the engine bay of any make or model of the automobile, scrape the grease off of a hidden bolt, and, using just my fingertips, tell you precisely what size socket or wrench you'll need to fetch to remove it. I can cook, sight in a brand new rifle with three shots, train a hunting dog, build a fire in the rain, and cut grade so smooth with a bulldozer you could roll a marble on it. But someone had to tell me that I was supposed to use the comma instead of the semicolon just then.

Although I did have a home with siblings, furniture, and parents in it, I didn't grow up there. I grew up at a deer camp. For anyone who isn't familiar with exactly what a deer camp is and thinks it's a place where people go to hunt deer and camp, let me explain:

First, a large tract of land is obtained by a group of hunters - usually, a lease because these typically aren't wealthy people who could afford to buy this much property. A board is formed among the leaseholders - a very organized board consisting of a president, vice president, secretary, treasurer, chairman, and so on. They decide on a piece of the property that will be the campsite, and this is where they are able to demonstrate the skills they have acquired throughout their lives as carpenters, electricians, plumbers, etc. They are a talented bunch. Once they have finished construction of their camp house or individual cabins (some nicer than their actual homes), they begin to work the land.

They must build roads, disk, and plant food plots, build stands, and spend thousands of dollars from a private checking account that their wives have no idea about just to have a place to go on the weekends to drink and play quarter-ante poker with the boys. When one of them does actually kill a deer, the others mutter bad things about him and his luck and lack of skill as a hunter, as if killing a deer was never supposed to happen. A motley group they are, but some of the best men I've ever had the pleasure of meeting.

There are many strange rituals and traditions carried out at camp. One is cutting the shirttail of a fellow hunter when he shoots and misses a deer. The hunter is then ridiculed and has to buy a new shirt. This can be avoided during bow season because the hunter can just lie and say that he hasn't seen anything since a bow is virtually silent, and nobody will know. That is, as long as he is a smart hunter and uses a nearby creek to wash the dirt off of his arrow to avoid detection by the keen eyes of the other, smarter hunters. This comes only through years of experience. Another is celebrating a youngster's first deer by smearing the blood on his or her face. Native Americans would wear the blood of an animal to pay respect to the animal and the fact that sometimes things had to die in order for something else to live. That same lesson is taught here and will pay off as the child grows older and gains a perspective on life and death. And my God, those men can cook.

The fire, the grill, and the pot are where stories are told. While the kids get to watch their elders prepare foods that usually aren't on the menu at home, they also get to hear all the tales from the old days. While a lot of these stories may challenge the boundaries of fact (and some old men can tell some whoppers), another valuable lesson is taught here: never interrupt people when they are talking. A typical conversation between two or more people who were never taught this is similar to being in a car that's spinning out of control; you have no idea where it's going, but you sure can't wait for it to stop.

So, it's a very unique place to grow up. It's a place where morals aren't forced upon you the way they are in church but made into fun and interesting rungs on the ladder of manhood. You learn how to drive here, and you learn directions, both in and out of the woods, as well as direction in life. And when the day comes that you are accepted into the group of men, they no longer say, "he's a good kid" or "he's a good hunter." You become an "outdoorsman."

The Outdoorsman

He is altogether a different breed of human being. He is deeply spiritual and very passionate about nature. The outdoorsman sees God through His Creation, the correlation between plant and animal, the artwork of the sky and the earth, and the natural attraction we all have to the dirt that we came from. There is a certain way his eyes move when something demands his attention; they don't dart around wildly; they are slow, sweeping back and forth just in front of his head movement. His eyes are calm; his soul is calm. Throughout the months of hunting season, those eyes are fixed on something very far away, most of the time something that's not even there. They scan the horizon for ducks, the edge of a field for deer, or the canopy of an oak tree waiting for the flicker of a squirrel's tail. His eyes move slowly, and his motions even slower. The knowledge that both the hunter and the *hunted* possess is that they are both being watched. They both know that stealth and attention to minor detail are the two key ingredients to their success, and the first to be seen is the loser of the game.

The true outdoorsman is a lover of life, all life. He stops his truck to help a turtle get across the street. He thinks that a nest full of baby birds is nothing less than adorable, but he also hunts. He takes great pride in having the skills to venture out into the wilderness and harvest an animal to supply food for his family and friends. But he doesn't have a darkened heart that causes him to feel joy simply from the experience of killing. A young hunter who has not yet been educated in what the pursuit of wild game is all about may feel a strange sense of pleasure from his or her first few kills. This is partly because of all the praise they receive from fellow hunters and also because that's just the nature of the beasts that we are. That feeling has to be tamed. The love and respect for nature must be taught by that child's elders. The survival of our species is no longer dependent on the ability to hunt and forage for our food. We are in the age of agriculture. But without this respect for God and Nature, we are going to destroy this planet.

I've heard people say that some land is overpopulated with deer and that the herd must be thinned by over half to produce "healthy genetics." I would argue that as long as the deer are healthy and free of disease, the genetics are just fine. There are certainly times when population management is essential to the health of the deer because of disease and shortage of food. But killing things off en masse simply for looks is exactly what Adolf Hitler was most famous for. Are those hunters aware that their philosophy of managing a species was already thought of? This may sound extreme because I'm comparing animals to humans, and mostly good people to a murdering psychopath, but calling this act proper management is vulgar and arrogant.

Genesis 1:28 says: "And God blessed them, and God said unto them, be fruitful and multiply, and replenish the earth, and subdue it: and have dominion over the fish of the sea, and over the fowl of the air, and over every living thing that moveth upon the earth."

God gave us the gift of life and the whole world to have to live. But with those gifts comes the responsibility of taking care of them. For example, when you were a teenager, your parents went out of town and expected you to look after their home because they trusted you. But you threw a party and trashed it because power and free will can be used as weapons in the hands of people who aren't careful.

So, backing up to the word "subdue" in the scripture, what was God instructing man to do with the earth? To subdue could mean to control, to cultivate, or to conquer. To conquer the earth and destroy it is obviously how a lot of people understood it, but we know that isn't right. Controlling it is a somewhat feasible task, but control is power over something, and that could wind up in the wrong hands. I think He wanted us to cultivate the earth to take care of and manage it, to live with the earth and not just on it, not to seek vengeance for life on it simply because of it living too well, and not to exploit the earth and mine it of all of its resources. People who were raised to be outdoorsmen know that taking out selected targets of the herd is the key to proper management. They also understand that taking care of the land is taking care of humanity.

It is the pursuit of the trophy that has destroyed the integrity of the deer hunter. I have never heard, and will never hear of, a duck hunter say that he has too many ducks on his property and that they need to be eradicated. The reason is that they all look the same, or, at least, each species of duck, separately. A duck in winter, in its full plumage, is one of the most beautiful things in the natural world. But the duck, unlike the bull elk or whitetail buck, doesn't carry a set of antlers. Conservation efforts are made to restore habitat and factor our daily bag limits, much like the deer. Wildlife biologists determine how many animals need to be harvested each year to maintain a healthy population. This determination is based on numbers, not hypothetical theories. They are also based on the management of a species as a whole, not the size of the antlers. Hunters undermine the work of these professionals when they attempt to micromanage what is already being done the right way.

I have stood knee-deep in a flooded rice field at sunrise and watched 50,000 ducks rise into the air at once and paint the entire sky black. I stood there and watched, in shock and awe, the breathtaking beauty of what was taking place in front of me, and I shared that moment with the closest friends I had. There were three men with three shotguns that each held three shells, and none of us even thought of firing a shot. We aren't killers. One shot alone could have easily knocked down twenty birds, but where is the challenge in that? That would have sent us over our possession limit and cost us a hefty fine, made for a pitiful excuse of a story to tell other hunters, and scared the birds out of the area so that the next man and his grandson wouldn't have the opportunity to experience that magic. What we did was sit there in silence, grinning ear to ear for about ten minutes until they were gone, then called a few back in at a time. We shot eight birds that morning, then went home, invited some friends over to tell them about the hunt, and feasted on some of the best gumbo I've ever eaten. I've been doing this since 1994, and in all those years of chasing ducks across the state, I have limited out more times than I can count. I shot two ducks that morning: a bull pintail and a green-winged teal. That was by far the best hunt I have ever been on.

I have bagged over one hundred deer in my lifetime; I'm 38 years old. That's an average of three and a half deer per season since taking my first one at age 9. I usually butcher one myself, have one processed into sausage and burger, and give one or two away to people who aren't fortunate enough to get one for themselves. The state quota for deer in Mississippi is eight. If I ever needed more meat for the freezer, the door was open for me to get it. I have one buck on my wall. He isn't there for bragging rights. He was my first mature buck and not a giant by most people's measure. But he sure was a giant to me at 11 years old, and by having him mounted, I'm able to relive the hunt in that swamp that December with my daddy every time I look at him.

People who kill things just for the sake of killing have no place in the tribe of outdoorsmen. They don't have the skills required to be welcomed into that circle, so they cheat with spotlights and illegal use of baiting. They aren't trained to be still and to be patient; they are restless. They were never taught to love nature, so they trample it and leave their trash behind. Those are the people who give the rest of us a bad image with animal rights activist groups.

I'm not as self-righteous and arrogant as this all may sound. I'm also not a hypocrite. The reason that I detest this person is because I used to be this person. I've seen the destruction it causes from the grandstands as well as from inside the arena. I was raised better and knew it was wrong, but I did it anyway. I am a living testimony of how badly the act of killing in vain can destroy a man's soul. It hardened me, and I soon found myself surrounded by the type of people that one should not dare call friends. I became a violent person, one with no understanding of what it means to be a man. My real friends faded away into the protection of their own lives that didn't involve them with outlaws. I lost friends, girlfriends, and the opportunity to play professional baseball, but worst of all, my relationship with Christ. The only thing I didn't lose was my family, and I think that they were just hanging on because they knew that I was raised by people with some decency, so surely I had some in there somewhere. When I stopped killing everything in my life (animate and inanimate) and decided to live the life I once had with God in it, almost everything good was resurrected and came back to me. It was that simple.

Now, my conversations are soft, my movements are slow and measured, my footsteps are light, my hands are steady, and my eyes are true. There is sereneness inside of me. I am at peace with myself and the world around me, and that old hunter's spirit is alive and doing well. My soul is tempered by love and raging with it at the same time. I am on a mission to preserve the good life.

The Man of Steel

I want to tell you a story about my grandfather, the greatest man I ever knew.

One day in the winter of 1993, we were sitting at the top of a big ridge that overlooked a hardwood bottom filled with white oak trees dropping acorns. He wasn't the "trophy hunter" type that you see on television with calls and other gadgets dangling around his neck like Mardi Gras beads; he was a meat hunter. Born in 1934, he grew up during the times when deer in Mississippi weren't as plentiful and required much more skill to hunt successfully. He didn't really care that much about the size of a deer's antlers, but to say he didn't care at all just isn't true. He just never was the guy who would pass up a shot at an eight-point with hopes of shooting a ten-point. He said to me many times, "Boy, you can't eat the horns."

Every deer I remember him ever seeing, whether it was in the woods or on the side of the road, excited him like it was the first one he'd ever seen. I guess it was a combination of his love for the beauty of this animal and how good they tasted fried with biscuits and gravy that compelled him to always fire every single bullet his gun held.

So we're sitting on this ridge when a buck walks out about a hundred yards away. Before I had a chance to cover my ears, that old Remington of his was howling; it sounded like a war zone. A model 7400 Remington 30.06 holds five rounds: one in the chamber and four in the magazine. After his fifth round struck God knows what and the rifle was empty, barrel smoking, he was still pulling the trigger and grinning like a possum. I was completely mortified and shaking all over.

Giving the animal no time to lie down and die in peace, we were quickly on his trail. Up and down the big hills, we went deeper and deeper into the woods of Wilkinson County, Mississippi, in search of this deer. We found it lying at the bottom of a deep ravine, dead as country music; a nice seven-point. But instead of going down to admire the animal as a hunter is known to do, his excitement had turned to worry. I had seen illegal deer before and was sure that this one met all of the legal standards, so I was a little confused by this. He said to me, "Come on, let's go get some help," then handed me the key to his Honda Big Red three-wheeler and told me to drive us back to camp.

When we pulled into camp, he had me drop him off at a man's cabin and told me to go fetch my daddy and get his deer out of the woods. The two men then drove away to what I would later find out was the hospital. My grandfather had suffered a heart attack but was able to maintain the strength and self-composure to make it out of the woods and hide it from his ten-year-old grandson to keep from scaring him. But it didn't kill him; neither did the next one: the Korean War, the tornado in 1966 where he laid on top of my mother and her two sisters to protect them, the stroke he suffered in 1998, a whole list of different types of cancer; or the lightning bolt that struck him in his own front yard. He was a true man of steel but with a heart as soft as a down comforter.

Life at camp went back to normal once we got the news that he was going to be alright. We got his deer out of the woods after my daddy scratched his head for a while in wonder at the sight of this animal that, in his words, was "shot all to hell." He asked me how many times he shot, and I pulled five empty hulls out of my coveralls that I collected off the ground. Everybody got a kick out of that.

We named that deer "Heart Attack," and although he was much smaller than other deer that have been given that same name, his story is just as big and told with great passion. The way we tell it varies from time to time, but the best version stretches the truth a bit and ends with the deer succumbing to heart failure rather than multiple gunshot wounds; the slightest of embellishment - Another campfire story born.

"Heart Attack"

God's Country

We had a little over 3,000 acres of land at the deer camp that sat on a peninsula between three rivers: the Homochitto, the Buffalo, and the Mississippi. There was a 400-acre cypress swamp that very few people, other than those of the Natchez Indian tribe, have ever stepped foot in. There were wild plum and pecan trees scattered throughout the place, and every one of the forty-plus members could walk you right up to the base of each one. I was wandering around by myself in the woods one summer (back then, kids could be trusted not to pick up rattlesnakes or jump off cliffs) and found an ancient oak tree with carvings of deer, wild boar, and fish in it. I assume this was the work of the aforementioned tribe. So much history was hidden away in this place, including the grave of Jefferson Davis' little sister behind an old church, right off of the main road on the west bank of Steele Creek.

When you're that young (I was only twelve when the landowner sold it out from under us), you take things like this for granted. Children don't understand the true value of things in life, and, unfortunately, neither do most adults. I think everyone understood it on the last day when we all packed up for the last time and said goodbye to each other. I saw more honest tears shed that day than I've ever seen at a funeral.

It's been 25 years since I've walked those sacred grounds, and I can still remember every square inch of it, as well as the names and faces of each member. Sills Hunting Club will always hold a very special place in the heart of any person who knows of its existence. Some of those men and women have gone on to receive their reward in the Kingdom of Heaven, while others still talk to each other every day. Some just kind of faded away and lost touch with the ones who were such a big part of their lives through the 80's and 90's. Every one of them has at least one outrageous story attached to their name.

It was these people who taught me how to "smell the rain." Even if you can't smell it, you can see the leaves on the trees flip over in the breeze and show their white underside, and you know that rain is surely coming. These good folks shared all of the country's wisdom they had learned from the ones before them with us kids at camp. We were taught respect and manners and how to just be decent people, but also given a wealth of knowledge and a love for The Great Outdoors.

When the wind blows constantly for at least three days out of the northwest in mid-November, you can expect the first big arrival of migrating ducks to appear in the days to follow. The first full moon of December in south Mississippi means that, no matter how busy you are, it's time to drop whatever you're doing and make your way into the woods because that big buck you've been after since bow-season is about to let his guard down in search of a hot doe. The rut is on. The bark that you saw rubbed off those little saplings a month or two ago could have been any buck, large or small, just scratching the last bit of velvet off of his antlers. This shouldn't be confused with the rubs you are seeing now on much larger trees, as those same bucks are strengthening their neck muscles, preparing to fight for territory and breeding rights. Do look closely at the shavings on the ground and their shape; thin, stringy ones come from the tiny knobs at the base of the antlers of a deer, while the wider shavings could be from a mean ol' boar hog sharpening his tusks. This is very useful knowledge.

When the gray squirrels are seen burying acorns in random places across the forest floor, you know that winter may be cold and harsh. The squirrel knows that if food becomes scarce, other hungry animals will surely commit larceny and rummage through their caches in order to survive. This act of storing food in multiple places will better the squirrel's odds of survival. Apply this knowledge to the way you store food at home: can some, freeze some, and dehydrate some. And when an old person tells you not to go down in such and such woods or not to go across such and such creek, well, buddy, they mean it. To do so anyway would make you a total fool. The old folks know. If they tell you that a duck can pull a truck, you'd better hitch it up.

Preparing Wild Game for the Table

Venison:

There is a bad habit among hunters that hurts me to even talk about. When I see one do this horrific thing in person, I cringe, shudder, lose all self-control, and have a visceral reaction that is similar to Speaker of the House Nancy Pelosi when she hears the mention of the name Donald Trump. It drives me crazy. I don't know when people started doing this, and I don't care. All I know is that I have tried explaining to people many times how wrong this act is, and it just goes in one ear and out the other. It is the number one deadly sin of handling fresh venison, or any meat, for that matter. If you are one of these many people, then I beg you to please stop putting meat into a cooler full of ice and water.

The idea that soaking deer meat in water takes the "gamey" flavor out may be true, and that's because it takes the *entire* flavor out. What you are left with is a blank canvas to cook with that is only going to taste like whatever you choose to season it with. Is that what you do with a steak? Did this animal give its life to someone who eats it and thinks it tastes bad? You can go down to the local meat market or neighborhood grocery store, pick up meat that was raised on a farm and fed grain for most of its life, and a lot of times, it will cost much less than it does to go hunting.

Deer are ruminants. They are grass eaters. They love other things, too, like acorns, wild berries, the peas you just planted, etc. But their bodies are designed to convert grass into protein. Their meat is very good for you and very tasty if you don't marinate it in tap water. But grass-fed meat can be a little tough when eaten fresh if the animal wasn't finished on grain before its slaughter. This grain-finishing is where you get all of the pretty fat marbling in beef. The beef industry has been doing this for a long time, mainly because it's cheaper to feed the cows corn to bring them up to slaughter weight than grass and then bypass the dry-aging process, the process that makes red meat taste oh-so-fine. So, unless you can lasso a deer, open it up, and feed it corn for the final 3-4 months of its life (which is illegal, so you shouldn't), then the meat needs to be dry-aged for at least five days, but preferably 7-10.

If you are one of the few people who are fortunate enough to have access to a walk-in cooler, then this is a very easy task. Once your deer has been dressed and all organs, scent glands, and head removed, cut all the way down to the throat, being sure to split the breastbone. Rinse out the chest cavity with water, then transfer to the walk-in and hang for about one week. Once the deer has hung for the allotted time, you can peel off the hide with ease and begin the butchering process. The meat will now be a much darker color, be very tender, and taste much better than it did when it was freshly killed. But if you don't have the luxury of a walk-in cooler, you can still achieve this goal, just on a smaller scale.

Take your choice cuts (roasts and steaks), trim them of all silver skin and other tissue, and lay them out on a table where you have plenty of room to work. Dry the meat well with paper towels and place them in a container. Wrap each piece of meat individually with three layers of paper towels and place in another container, uncovered, in the refrigerator. After two days, you will need to remove all paper towels and re-wrap them with three more layers. Be sure not to crowd them all together in the container. The goal is for cold air to swirl all around the meat and somewhat dry it. This will make the meat very tender, tastier, and very juicy when you cook it; a paradox that I can't explain, but it works. Repeat this two more times, giving the aging process a total time of six days in the refrigerator, then cook or freeze.

If you plan to have your venison processed into sausage or other things that use lots of seasoning, then this dry-aging can be skipped. Not that it doesn't matter because there is a noticeable difference, but it doesn't change that much. But if you plan on cooking a roast or steaks grilled to a beautiful medium and serving them to your friends, please don't put the meat in water and spoil the wonderful flavors.

Waterfowl:

It is so simple to break out a duck or a goose by taking your thumb and running it up the breastbone to remove a thin line of feathers, then cutting away the meat. You will be left with a nice boneless filet of breast meat to use in a ton of recipes. We often do this because the birds can be hard to pluck, and the rest of the birds don't yield very much meat. But the flavor in fowl is in places other than the breast, mainly the thighs and back.

An easy way to remove the feathers is by scalding the bird first in hot water. The feathers will then be very easy to remove. Take a large pot, such as the one you would use for frying a turkey or even one for boiling shrimp or crawfish, fill it with water, and bring it to a boil on an outdoor cooker. Holding the bird by its head, submerge it in the boiling water for 15-20 seconds up to its neck. A short stick or a large pair of tongs works great to keep the bird down in the water so it doesn't just float on the surface. Once the bird has cooled, the feathers should be easy to remove. If not, just dip it in the water again for another 15 seconds.

Take your plucked bird and cut an incision at the base of the breastbone in a circle, all the way around to the tailbone. Use poultry shears to cut through the thin tailbone to remove. The oil glands at the base of the tailbone can give off-flavors in cooking. Reach inside the bird and pull out all of the entrails and other organs, using your fingers to scrape the lungs free from the rib cage. Once this is done, you can sometimes remove the head and neck with a firm tug. You may need to do a little work with a knife around the neck, but try not to damage the skin at the top of the breast. Remove the legs at the knuckle just below the feather line, rinse out the cavity to remove any bone fragments, and you now have a duck or goose perfectly prepared for roasting.

If you only prefer to eat the breast meat of the bird, you can still remove them to use in your recipe. But now you have the remainder of the bird to make a very delicious stock for a variety of other things.

For a Simple Stock:

Place duck carcass in a pan in the oven at 300°F for about 1 hour. Add 8 cups of water to an 8-quart stockpot and bring to a boil. Add the roasted duck carcass, two yellow onions (quartered), 3 stalks of celery (cut into thirds), 3-4 large carrots (cut into chunks, 2 bay leaves, 2 cloves of garlic, and 1 teaspoon of black peppercorns. Reduce to a low simmer and cook, uncovered, for 2 ½ hours. You will need to skim the fat off the top with a spoon periodically as the stock simmers.

Strain through a fine-mesh sieve and discard all solids. Return stock to the pot and simmer for 1 ½ hours, skimming any fat off the top. The end result should be the color of beef stock: dark in color but not cloudy.

*This is just an example of how to make a basic stock, the one I use for gumbo. You can make as much as you want by adding more of each ingredient, taking away, or adding new ones. Dial it in for yourself and make it personal.

*See "The Foundations of Creole and Cajun Cooking"

Cooking with Cast-Iron

Cast iron is more than just novelty cookware; it is practical and essential in getting some foods to cook just right. Folks down here don't cook everything in cast iron, contrary to popular belief. But it can fry chicken extremely well, and it also gives biscuits and cornbread a nice brown bottom. The cast iron holds heat well, and the dark color helps brown the food better than lighter-colored pans. If you prefer a lighter, softer biscuit, then use a 9-inch cake pan. I do.

But if I could have only one pan to cook with, it would definitely be cast-iron, a 10-inch skillet, to be exact. If seasoned properly, the thing will outlast most family names. By "seasoned," I mean that it has absorbed enough grease to keep food from sticking, but it will also keep the pan from drying out and rusting as well.

Sometimes, you may need to clean the pan from years of being used. This is acceptable as long as it's not your grandma's cornbread pan. Rinse it well in hot water, a couple of drops of dishwashing liquid, and one of those little scrubber sponges with the scouring pad on one side. Any bits stuck on the bottom can usually be scraped off with just the help of water and a plastic spatula. If it is just absolutely filthy, then you can use fine steel wool for finishing, but nothing too abrasive. When the pan is clean, dry it well with a towel and rub 2 tablespoons of canola oil and 1 tablespoon of bacon grease all over the inside and outside of the pan, as well as on the handle. Rub oil in real good with paper towels, removing any excess. Place the pan upside down on the middle rack of a 450°F oven and leave for 4 hours. The heat will expand the metal, and as it cools, the metal contracts and traps the grease in its pores.

There is no limit to how many times you can do this. You cannot "over-season" a cast-iron skillet. Cooking acidic foods like tomatoes can strip the pan of its seasoning, so avoid using cast iron for dishes that use these ingredients and cook for a long time. The metal will also react with the acid and give the food a bad taste.

So, let's keep this simple: Use cast iron primarily for bread and meat dishes. Fried potatoes are wonderful when cooked in a cast-iron skillet with butter and sliced onions, but they can stick and burn very easily. Most desserts are slightly acidic, but when cooking things like cobblers or pineapple upside-down cake, there is no substitute for a heavy, black, grease-soaked cast-iron skillet.

Camp Food

The food that people eat when they go camping can vary from gas station sardines with crackers all the way to five-star cuisine. The top ten meals I've ever eaten have all been while camping somewhere far away from civilization. That's because we have no boundaries to the way we cook. Nobody is there to tell you things like how runny to leave their eggs or how far to cook the steak. You just kind of do what you want. Most of the time, when people are camping, they stay pretty active and burn more calories than usual, especially when it's cold, so the food has a different taste because you can go a little heavier on fat and calories.

The proper way to cook breakfast at home, by frying bacon in one skillet and scrambling eggs in another while the biscuits cook in the oven so it is all ready at the same time, is absolutely unacceptable while at camp. You fry the bacon and pour the grease into a quart-sized mason jar for later use, but leave a little bit in the skillet, and then you scramble the eggs in the bacon grease, take the bacon and eggs and put them in a pan and stick it in the oven. Turn the oven to 450°F and very quickly make biscuits, using some of your reserved bacon grease to coat the pan. Biscuits take about 12 minutes to cook at this temperature. At the halfway mark, remove bacon and eggs from the oven and make your plates. As soon as the biscuits come out, slather them with butter and serve. The entire meal will be at the right temperature, and it will taste like Heaven. Go walk it off.

An old man by the name of Joel Brown taught me how to properly make biscuits when I was about fourteen years old. He taught me how to wipe the skillet with just enough grease but not too much because it fries the bottoms. He taught me the word "slather" and how to do it with real butter because that's what makes 'em good. Daddy taught me how to use the grill and how to not go all crazy with the flippin', to just let the grill do the work. This is a high honor among men and one that I was very proud of when they let me cook the food.

Buttermilk Biscuits

3 cups White Lily self-rising flour,

1 stick cold butter, cubed

1 cup cold buttermilk

How to make biscuits is one of the most controversial subjects you will hear discussed in a Southern kitchen. Just the term "cathead" is the groundwork for a heated debate between two people who have worn out more ovens than most folks have shoes. One of them may say that it means the biscuits are as big as the head of a cat, while the other one argues that the triangular shape of a hand-tossed biscuit is the shape of the head of a cat. Both are true. That argument may then switch to whether it is best to use self-rising flour or all-purpose with baking powder and soda. Then to oven temperature, outside humidity, what sign of the zodiac that particular day is in, and just about any other tiny adjustment that could be made to change the taste or texture of a biscuit, all of which are worthy of one's attention.

I believe that a cathead biscuit is one that isn't rolled and cut but handmade and placed in the pan in a rough shape, the triangular one. It doesn't really matter. What matters is how much love you put into making them. Are your biscuits simply going to be the stage for a store-bought jelly or package of "country gravy" mix? Or are they going to be the centerpiece that is highlighted by a good homemade jam, jelly, or gravy? If it's the former, then go out and buy yourself a can of tube biscuits, whop 'em on the counter, lay them in a pan, and tickle someone's belly. If it's authenticity you want and a light, fluffy, perfect biscuit, then roll up your sleeves and make them yourself.

How you handle the dough is just as important as the recipe you follow. If you make the dough too wet, the biscuit will be crumbly and won't rise well. Too stiff, and you will need a good-quality hammer and chisel to eat one. But if you over-mix your dough, then it doesn't matter what recipe you use; your biscuits will be unfit to eat.

You have the option of using a cutter for a perfectly round biscuit that is layered and great for splitting apart and spreading jam or jelly on. You don't need a rolling pin; you just need to lay the dough out on a lightly floured surface, pat it out to ½-¾ inch thick, fold it in half, then pat it back out to 1 inch thick. Take a 3-inch cutter or a drinking glass, dip it in a pile of flour so the dough won't stick to it, and cut out your biscuits. Do not twist when you cut; twisting will seal the edges and ruin those nice layers. Lay them in the pan, leaving about ½ inch between each one.

The second option is to flour your hands well, reach into the bowl of dough, pinch off a chunk, toss it back and forth in your hands to form a rough-shaped ball, and lay it straight into the greased pan. When you make them this way, you don't want any space left between the biscuits the way you would leave with the cut ones. The biscuits will rise as one but break apart easily when done, leaving very soft edges. These "cathead" biscuits are what you would typically serve with gravy.

For the Dough:

Combine cubed butter with flour and mix, by hand, until all butter is incorporated into the flour and the mixture is crumbly. Add buttermilk to flour, again mixing with hands until a shaggy dough has formed, and then set aside.

Preheat oven to 450°F. Lightly grease a 10-inch cast-iron skillet with 1 tablespoon of bacon grease, being sure to coat the sides and bottom evenly. Add biscuits to the skillet in a ring, with the last one going in the center. Very lightly press the biscuits down so all of the tops are of even height to prevent uneven browning. Place on the middle rack of the oven and bake for 14-16 minutes, or until tops are light, golden brown. Serve hot.

Sawmill Gravy

1 lb pork breakfast sausage

¼ cup all-purpose flour

¾ stick unsalted butter

3 cups whole milk

Salt and pepper

In a large skillet, cook sausage over low-medium heat, breaking it apart as it cooks. Drain most of the grease, add butter, and bring back up to a low simmer. Add ¼ cup of flour directly to the skillet and cook, stirring constantly, until flour has combined, about 2-3 minutes. Stir in milk, about 1 cup at a time, stirring constantly to prevent lumps from forming. You may not use all 3 cups of milk; just keep adding until the gravy has reached your desired thickness. If it gets too thin, a little extra heat should thicken it some. Add salt and plenty of black pepper to taste and serve over hot biscuits.

Venison Stew

2lbs venison tenderloin, cut into bite-size pieces

2 qts beef broth

4 russet potatoes

1 celery stalk, chopped

3 large carrots, cut ½ inch thick

2 yellow onions, quartered

4 cloves garlic, crushed

1 qt stewed tomatoes with juice

1 pt tomato juice

3 Tbsp all-purpose flour

3 Tbsp bacon grease

1 Tbsp salt

1 Tbsp black pepper

2 bay leaves

In a large pot over medium heat, add beef broth, celery, onions, and carrots. Let simmer for 30 minutes, then add stewed tomatoes, garlic, and bay leaves.

In a mixing bowl, toss venison in ¼ cup of flour to coat well. Heat the bacon grease in a large cast-iron skillet over medium heat and brown meat well on all sides. Add tomato juice to the skillet to deglaze, scraping all browned bits from the bottom with a spatula.

Add meat, potatoes, salt, and pepper to the pot. Cover with a lid, reduce heat to a very low simmer, and cook for 1 hour. Remove bay leaves and serve in bowls.

Hamburger Steak with Gravy

1lb ground beef

1 white onion, thinly sliced

2 cloves garlic, crushed

3 Tbsp butter

1 ½ cups whole milk

2 Tbsp all-purpose flour

1 Tbsp bacon grease

1 Tbsp Dale's marinade

Salt and pepper

Heat 1 Tbsp of bacon grease in a cast-iron skillet over medium heat. Add a little salt and pepper to the meat and form into ½-¾ inch thick patties. Fry patties on each side until done, then set aside.

Add butter to the skillet. Let butter sizzle until it starts to brown a little, then add onions and garlic. Cook until onions are very soft. Add flour to skillet and cook for about 3 minutes, until it all starts to bind together. Start by adding milk ¼ cup at a time and whisking all the lumps out until a nice gravy has formed. Add 1 Tbsp of Dale's marinade, then return the meat and let simmer in the gravy for about 5 minutes. If some of the meat breaks apart, then you have successfully recreated this dish just as the old men at camp used to make it. Serve over white rice.

Bacon-Wrapped Tenderized Steaks

1lb good bacon

2lbs tenderized venison or beef steaks

1 (8oz) package cream cheese

1 (20oz) bottle of Italian dressing

2 large jalapeno peppers, seeded and cut into thin strips

1 small jar of fig preserves

Salt and lemon pepper

Marinate steaks in a bowl of Italian dressing in the refrigerator for 24 hours. Remove meat and discard marinade. Pat steaks dry with paper towels and lightly season each side with lemon pepper and salt.

On each steak, add 1 Tbsp cream cheese, 1 tsp of fig preserves, and a thin strip of jalapeno pepper, then roll up and wrap tightly with a whole strip of bacon. Be sure to wrap the bacon all the way to the ends to keep the filling from melting out. Secure with toothpicks and grill slowly for about 20 minutes or until bacon is crispy.

Duck and Sausage Gumbo

1 cup all-purpose flour

1 cup canola oil

6 cups duck stock (for a lighter taste, use chicken stock)

8 wood duck breasts, skins removed and cubed

1lb andouille sausage, cut ¼ inch thick

2 white onions, chopped

1 cup chopped green bell pepper

1 cup chopped celery

4 cloves garlic, crushed

1 cup okra, cut ¼ inch thick

1 Tbsp dried thyme

1 Tbsp onion powder

1 Tbsp garlic powder

1 tsp paprika

1 tsp gumbo filé powder

1 tsp black pepper

1 tsp white pepper

1 tsp cayenne pepper

¼ cup chopped fresh parsley

¼ cup chopped fresh green onion 3 bay leaves

1 Tbsp Tabasco sauce

1 tsp salt

Brown duck in a skillet, then set aside. In a large pot, heat oil over medium-high heat. Whisk flour into the hot oil. After the sizzling has settled, lower the heat to medium and continue whisking until the roux has turned to dark chocolate brown for about 25 minutes. Add onions and continue to cook for another 5 minutes, being careful to keep stirring and not burn the roux.

Add sausage, celery, bell pepper, garlic, and okra. Add 1 cup of stock and whisk to combine. Add all remaining stock and bay leaves, and then reduce heat to a low simmer. Cook for 20 minutes.

Add duck and all remaining ingredients and let cook for another 20 minutes. Add salt if needed and more Tabasco if desired; remove bay leaves and serve over white rice.

Camp-Style Barbecue Beans

1 lb dried pinto beans

1 medium white onion, chopped

1 green bell pepper, chopped

4 slices of good bacon, chopped

1 cup tomato sauce

½ cup molasses

3 Tbsp dark brown sugar

1 Tbsp tomato paste

1 Tbsp chili powder

1 tsp black pepper

1 tsp salt

1 tsp dried mustard powder

Soak beans in cold water overnight or at least 12 hours. Discard water.

In a medium pot over medium heat, cook pinto beans in enough clean water to cover by 2 inches until done but not mushy, about 50 minutes. Do not drain.

In a skillet, cook bacon until crispy. Toss in onion and bell pepper and continue cooking until vegetables begin to soften. Combine all ingredients in a disposable aluminum pan, mix well, and then cover with foil.

If you are already grilling or smoking and have space for the beans, they will do fine there. An easy way is to place them on the middle rack of the oven and cook for 1 hour at 350°F.

*A smoker generally cooks at a low temperature and could require a longer cooking time.

Ham Steaks with Redeye Gravy

5 ham steaks, cut ¼ inch thick

2 cups strong black coffee

3 Tbsp dark brown sugar

In a large cast-iron skillet over medium heat, fry ham steaks until nicely browned on each side. Remove ham and set aside, reserving drippings in the skillet.

In a bowl, combine coffee and brown sugar. Pour coffee into a hot skillet with reserved drippings and scrape browned bits from the bottom with a spatula. Bring to a boil and cook, stirring occasionally, until the liquid is reduced to half, give or take a little. Pour the gravy over ham steaks and serve with hot biscuits.

Chapter 2
The Grandparents:

We called my grandfather "Baw Baw." My brother, Cory, apparently couldn't say "Paw Paw" when he was young, so it just kind of stuck. We are all glad it did, too, because someone as unique and wonderful as Johnnie Middleton deserves their own custom handle. Baw Baw was my grandfather on my momma's side and the only one I ever really knew, being that the other one passed away when I was still too young to remember. Baw Baw was an outdoorsman, and he had bird dogs up until the 90s when the quail had all but disappeared, much like chivalry and well-behaved children. He built them a 24'x24' kennel in his backyard that was sectioned off so that each dog had its own space. It was built on a thicker slab of concrete than most houses are for humans and had a cyclone fence for a roof. He planted muscadine vines all around it, and as they grew to cover the top, they provided shade in the summer and sunshine in the winter once the leaves had fallen. It was brilliant.

I watched him train those dogs from tiny puppies into world-class pointers. They understood what he was telling them like he was talking to another person. If the dog was running around and being an idiot, he could give it the command to "hunt close," and the animal would instantly start making tight circles or zigzagging right out in front of the hunters. The dogs constantly looked back at the hunters to see where they were. Another command was "out front," telling the dogs to stay in front of the shooters and not behind them or off to the side. The reason for these commands was to prevent the dogs from flushing a bird that was out of shotgun range or, even worse, busting up a whole covey. If one pup pointed (a beautiful sight to see when that dog freezes in mid-stride like a statue, except for its tail vibrating from an uncontrollable level of excitement), then the other dog, or dogs, back it. To "back" another dog simply means to honor its point by pointing at him, alerting the shooter that they had fulfilled their duties, and now it's your turn. These were the best pointers and backers in the business: true hunting dogs. They weren't pets; they were working-class. But just like a lot of working-class people out there, these dogs had a few bad habits.

At a certain time of the year, late summer to be exact, those dogs would vacation from being well-disciplined, obedient hunters and howl non-stop every night until they went to sleep. My grandmother would tell us kids that they were howling at the moon, which, due to my wild imagination and Michael Jackson's newly released music video, "Thriller," made me think they might be werewolves, and that scared me a little. But Baw Baw, the less subtle of the two, would say that his prized hunting dogs had eaten the muscadines that had fallen into their kennel and fermented, were wound up tighter than Dick's hatband, and needed to go to rehab. Then he'd take them an entire loaf of bread that, according to him, was to "make 'em strong" tomorrow. I had no idea what any of that meant back then, but later in life, I did unlock the great mystery of fermented fruit. Here is the reason those dogs were always so eager to go back into their pen:

Homemade Muscadine Wine

Pick 10 gallons of ripe muscadines, scuppernongs, or both. I prefer a mixture of 80/20, mostly muscadines (the dark purple ones). Crush them well, and then separate them into two clean 5-gallon buckets. Add 5lbs of white sugar to each bucket, and then cover with a clean towel, tied tightly. Let the fruit work in a 60-75-degree area for about a week.

In another clean bucket, strain juice from worked-off fruit through a colander and then cheesecloth. You may be disappointed at how little juice comes out. This is a delicate thing to be served at gatherings such as Thanksgiving. You can squeeze the fruit and get a little more juice, but that makes the wine cloudy. I'm a man who prefers quality over quantity, and this is my wine recipe, so don't squeeze the damn things.

For every gallon of juice you have, add 2 lbs of sugar. Let work off for about a week or until it is done bubbling. Strain is really good. Now, for every gallon of juice, add 1lb of sugar. Let work off somewhere no warmer than 65°F and no less than 55°F until all bubbling stops. This final fermentation may take up to two weeks due to the lower temperature. This part is crucial, as warm temperatures could cause the wine to sour.

Do not strain the wine in the final step. If you have a siphon hose, siphon all but the last 3-4 inches of wine into a clean bucket. You could also dip the wine out by hand but still leave the last 3-4 inches. The bottom layer will have a little sediment and is very bitter to the taste buds, causing poor-quality wine.

Bottle your wine up and store it somewhere dark and cool, like you would any preserved food. And remember me telling you this. This is not the wine that you pass along to your friends who are snobs. There are no floral or spicy notes, no hints of oak, and as far as I'm concerned, it doesn't pair well with food. This stuff is delicious, but it tastes like it was run through a still.

Baw Baw and one of the men involved in the illegal meat trading scandal once went in half on a setter they named "Mr. Bojangles." The dog came with a small filing cabinet of paperwork, and although nobody in the family remembers what state he was purchased from, he actually was flown into Jackson International Airport from somewhere pretty far away. Just like all of Baw Baw's bird dogs, Mr. Bojangles was trained to perfection. He never developed the nasty habit of tracking quail by sniffing the ground; he hunted with his head held high. Two reasons a dog may do this, with only one of them being good: Either he is a prideful dog that is well aware of his pedigree and thinks he's better than other dogs. Or, he keeps his nose high so as not to track the bird's footsteps by sniffing the ground but smells for the bird itself. Heat rises, and a bird puts off a great deal of it. With that heat, a different scent rises than that of a bird that isn't there anymore. A good quail dog isn't a tracker; he uses all of the intelligence he can muster up to locate birds. When he points, what you see is the dog caught halfway between lunging at the quail and the restraint he has been taught not to scare or attack them.

Baw Baw used to hunt up in Ebenezer, Mississippi, for quail with a group of guys. One day, he decided he and Mr. Bojangles would take the trip up there for a one-on-one session to see what each other was made of. The dog crossed a road, and a truck came around the corner and hit him, killing him instantly. Baw Baw loaded him in the truck and brought him back home to bury him. When he came into the house that evening, he broke down right in my grandma's kitchen. No one had ever really seen him cry, and his only emotions were usually of happiness. So, after the family witnessed this man going through this much pain from the loss of his hunting companion, my grandmother told them all how much he paid for the dog. The wave of sympathy suddenly receded when they all realized he was more upset about the amount of money he lost that day. He always denied that, but he did it with that sideways look that a child gives when he's lying.

Nana

Mrs. Catherine Shirley Middleton came from Louisiana and brought style and flash to the table. Since I first started cooking, everything I've ever prepared has been an attempt to duplicate what she can do with food. That woman loved to cook, and she loved people, and that's the ticket to becoming great at this craft. That's what she taught me: love people, love to cook for people, and give all the glory to God.

Cooking is supposed to be fun, not just an arduous chore required to feed hungry people. I believe that the more we enjoy doing something, the more we strive to be good at it or even great. She was great at it. She could cook anything and make it taste the exact same way every time, no matter if it was done on a camp stove, on an open fire, or in the comfort of her own kitchen. Only legends can do that. She also garnished her food, which the majority of folks down here, up until about a decade or two ago, only saw as an obstacle in the way of their meal.

We called her "Nana," and Nana was a foodie in every true sense of that word. She used to scold my grandfather for his poor eating habits, telling him things like, "Johnnie, you have to eat something besides meat." Her concerns for people were for their overall health and happiness, and to her, both came from food. When I lived on the beach, I would try to visit at least once a month. Nana would tell me not to show up at her house without fresh shrimp, which I never did. I had a connection with a man who was a boat captain who specialized in catching the royal red shrimp in deep water. Royal reds are very delicate shrimp that are very easy to overcook if you don't know what you're doing. Not only did she know what she was doing, but she also turned a pound of sweet shrimp into the best chowder I have ever tasted. At 87, her best cooking days are behind her now. But she was an excellent teacher, which led to a few good cooks down the family line to carry out her legacy.

The grandparents complete the structure of a family. Their presence isn't as strong as the mother and father, and sometimes the grandchildren hardly see them at all, but the time spent with them has a very powerful effect. They offer the essential lessons in life and fill the gaps that our parents leave. Sometimes, the parents have a hectic schedule at work and can't be at home with the children every day. The grandparents take action; they babysit, take the kids to school, teach them how to cook, and debunk some of the myths in the child's mind.

I was boiling eggs one time at Nana's house for potato salad, and after completing the first two steps of placing the eggs in the pot and then pouring the cold water over them prior to cooking, I added a generous amount of salt to the water. Nana asked me why I added salt and then allowed me to give my reason. After telling her that it makes them easier to peel once they're cooked, she corrected me. According to her wisdom, the salt has no effect on the egg whatsoever. So we had a challenge. I cooked my eggs in one pot, and Nana cooked her eggs in another. My eggs went into the pot with the cold water over the top, her eggs the same. I salted my water, and she didn't. We cooked them for the same amount of time, then drained the hot water and rinsed them in cold water. But she left hers in the pot. Once mine were cool, I placed them into a colander and went to peeling. Hers just sat there while she helped to peel my eggs and told me a story. They were just as easy as every time, but just like most boiled eggs, some of the shells were hard to remove, and I even tore a few of the whites. When we got done peeling them, I had a bowl of 5 eggs, mostly intact. Nana began peeling hers under the water. Every egg was perfect. The salt had no effect, but leaving them in the water literally made the shells almost fall off on their own.

Nana and Baw Baw made life easy and fun. I learned so much from them, and we are all lucky to have had them in our lives. I think a big part of why us Southerners are skilled in areas such as the kitchen is because of all the teachers in our lives. I know some people who grew up in broken homes or ones who didn't have their grandparents and parents around, and they don't have the same skills. It blows their minds when you tell them things like "chickens don't need a rooster to produce eggs." This is a fact that anyone should know, that is, if they had someone to teach them. The truth is that about half of the people you talk to, especially the ones who didn't have a close relationship with their grandparents, have no idea that hens don't need a rooster to produce an egg. The absence of parents and grandparents may be one of the worst problems in this modern world and one more reason I treasure Southern culture. I couldn't imagine being raised without my grandparents around to teach me all about life when Mom and Dad couldn't.

Baw Baw and Nana

Grandma Turner

Daddy's mother, my Grandma Turner, could fry the best chicken in the world. She would serve it with rutabaga that had been boiled and mashed, then combined with sautéed onion and garlic and cooked in an iron skillet. Mashed potatoes aren't even in the same league. When she would raise the lid on the pot to stir her food, the intoxicating smells animated her kitchen and transformed her ordinary dining room into a table reserved only for resurrected kings and queens of past millennia. Born prior to the Great Depression, she grew up dirt-poor and learned an awful lot about life and hardships at a very young age. Her hands were worn and calloused from a lifetime of hard work as a grownup and from chopping cotton as a young girl. She was a very tough woman with a very straight forward approach to everything, especially her cooking. And I can't recall a single time that she ever missed church. If the doors were open, Grandma Turner was inside. About the only backsliding she ever did was swearing a little and dipping snuff on occasion. I wouldn't really call those sins, but I did hear my daddy say that she fired a round at him from a small caliber rifle one time. It missed, so I suppose that doesn't qualify either. That family had a strange obsession with shooting at each other. But I don't think Saint Peter would have locked the gate on her. If he did, then Heaven is surely lacking in the food department.

Miss Lucille Turner passed on from this world in the fall of 2014 at the ripe old age of 95. She left her children and grandchildren with the wisdom and skills to deal with any situation life throws at them. She taught us all how to see the beauty of simplicity and not be needy people, one of the greatest gifts I've ever received. She was a true woman of God, and when the day came that Heaven gained that angel, the Atlanta Braves lost their biggest fan.

Plainness and simplicity are the mainsprings of true happiness in this world. When one constantly wishes for things he or she may never acquire, they are staging a life of misery and longing. Lack of wanting is the key to achieving fulfillment in life, and that's what our grandparents stress as a lesson of utmost importance to us our entire lives. It's the little things that matter the most, like sitting on the porch and having a conversation or watching a ballgame on television. I wish I could still do that with them.

Some of my greatest childhood memories are of the time spent at my grandparents' houses. Baw Baw had a lake behind his house that was full of bass and bluegill. I spent most of my time in an old aluminum boat he had, learning all of the tricks to catching fish, tricks I still use to this day. One of those tricks is to use a porcupine quill as a bobber instead of a cork. Two tiny rubber bands slide up the line, and the quill is inserted into them, allowing you to slide it up and down the line to the preferred depth. The quill is very delicate and light and doesn't make much of a splash when you flip it under an old tree limb where the bream loves to bed. It doesn't require any kind of weight; the quill lays flat on the surface until the cricket on the hook pulls the line taught, where it will then stand up with the weight of the cricket. This offers a much more naturally presented bait to the fish, one that he has a really hard time resisting. I used to fill coolers full of fish over there.

Baw Baw and Nana lived in a neighborhood with about twenty-five houses around them. The houses were spread out but not really far enough for a child with a BB gun to wander around and shoot things. Grandma Turner lived inside the city limits, but her backyard was fenced in and big enough so that I could hone my shooting skills off of her back porch. This was my hunting grounds, and she even got rid of her scarecrow in the garden because I was the new sheriff in town, and all of the outlaw birds and squirrels had outstanding warrants. I eventually ran them all out of town with my trusty Benjamin 22 cal. The ones who didn't want to go peacefully got to meet their maker. Her garden was the bank, and they were the robbers.

Every Sunday, the family would gather at either grandparent's house to visit and eat dinner. The grandkids would climb trees and play in the dirt while the grownups prepared the meal, and by "meal," I mean feast. Most days, there would be about ten people visiting, so the food would be stacked high and always delicious. Grandparents keep really nice gardens, so the sides would mainly consist of whatever was growing at that particular time of year: true seasonal food. If they didn't grow it, then another gardener in the family or a neighbor did. They both had large standup, vault-like freezers at their houses and whatever they didn't freeze, they canned in mason jars and stashed all throughout the house. If a person couldn't develop a love for fresh, homegrown food in that environment, then they just never had a chance at it anywhere. But I guess when things like that are normal to someone because it's all they've ever known, it can be very easy to take for granted.

People who were born before 1950 can use the same ingredients, the same pots and pans, and the same methods of cooking as anyone else, and their food will taste better than the others every time. They have a special touch with things that come from a lifetime of correcting their mistakes. By the time their children have children and they become grandparents, they have honed the skills they possess to a razor's edge. Some of them are great storytellers, others great cooks, most of them both. I believe the greatest compliment a cook can get is when someone tells them that their food reminds them of something their mother or grandmother used to make. That's what good food is all about: that one bite that offers a person the pleasure of either a memory or something new and exciting. I hold the following recipes dear to my heart because, while very simple, they awaken those memories and take me back to the days when life was simple, and the only hard times were when a pack of drunken bird dogs kept us up all night.

Nana's Potato Salad

Boil (10 or so) potatoes in skins

Salt when boiling potatoes

1 jar med pimento

1 Tbsp vinegar

1 onion, diced fine

1/3 jar sweet pickles, diced fine

5 boiled eggs, chopped

Paprika, salt & pepper to taste

Mix in mayo

Nana passed away while I was writing this book, so I included this recipe because it is my favorite thing she made. I asked her for the recipe years ago, and this is exactly how the conversation went. It defines her cooking style to perfection.

Me: "How big a jar of pickles?"

  Nana: "You don't want the big one, just a regular jar."

Me: "It says here, 'mix in mayo.' How much mayo?"

  Nana: "You'll know when it's enough."

Me: "Russet potatoes or red potatoes?"

  Nana: "You don't eat the skin of a Russet potato."

Me; "I do."

      Nana: "You do a lot of things I don't approve of."

Baw Baw's Chili

3lbs ground beef

2 cups beef broth

2 cups tomato sauce

2 cups cooked kidney beans

1 ½ cups stewed tomatoes

1 large yellow onion, chopped

1 large green bell pepper, chopped

3 garlic cloves, crushed

3 Tbsp tomato paste

2 ½ Tbsp chili powder

2 tsp cumin

1 tsp ground coriander

½ tsp dried oregano

½ tsp cayenne pepper

Salt and pepper

In a medium pot over medium-high heat, cook ground beef until done, then set aside. Stir in beef broth and beans and bring to a boil. Reduce heat to a simmer and cook for 25 minutes, then add meat and all remaining ingredients. Cover with a lid and let simmer for 30 minutes. Add salt and pepper to taste and serve in bowls.

Grandma Turner's Fried Chicken

1 whole fryer chicken cut into 8 pieces

2 ½ cups buttermilk

3 cups all-purpose flour

1 Tbsp salt, plus 2 tsp

1 tsp garlic powder

1 tsp onion powder

½ tsp cayenne pepper

½ tsp paprika

½ tsp black pepper

½ tsp white pepper

2 cups vegetable oil

Wash the chicken pieces well, then transfer them to a large bowl of ice water and add 1 Tbsp of salt. Place in the refrigerator, covered for 2 hours.

Remove chicken and pat dry with paper towels. Rub 1 tsp of salt into the chicken and set aside. Combine buttermilk, garlic powder, onion powder, and black pepper in a large bowl, and then add chicken. Place in refrigerator, covered, for 10-12 hours.

In a large bowl, combine flour, 1 tsp salt, white pepper, cayenne pepper, and paprika. Remove chicken from the refrigerator and shake off excess buttermilk. Dredge each piece in flour and place on a plate. Put the floured chicken back into the refrigerator while you prepare to fry.

Heat 2 cups vegetable oil in a 12-inch cast-iron skillet over medium heat. Sprinkle a dash of flour into hot oil; if it sizzles, the oil is ready.

Lay each piece into the skillet, leaving at least a half inch of space between them. You may need to fry it in two separate batches.

Cover with a lid and fry for about 15 minutes on each side, turning only once. When the chicken is done, lay it on paper towels to drain.

Chicken Spaghetti

1 ½ pkg spaghetti

1 4-5lb whole fryer chicken

1 green bell pepper, chopped

2 large white onions, chopped

1 stalk celery, chopped

2 cloves garlic, minced

1 qt stewed tomatoes, drained

1 small can of sliced mushrooms

1 tsp salt

½ tsp black pepper

¼ tsp cayenne pepper

1 cup shredded cheddar

Butter

Boil the chicken until it is done, and shred it into pieces. In a skillet, heat 1 Tbsp butter over medium heat and cook onion until it begins to soften. Add celery and bell pepper and cook until soft. Toss in garlic and tomatoes and cook for about 20 minutes.

Cook spaghetti until tender, then drain and set aside. Butter a casserole dish and preheat oven to 350°F. Combine all ingredients, mix well, and pour the mixture into the casserole dish. Top with cheese and bake, uncovered, for 25 minutes.

Meatloaf

2lbs lean ground beef

1 medium white onion, finely chopped

2 Tbsp finely chopped green bell pepper

2 large eggs

2 cloves garlic, minced

¼ cup tomato sauce

4 slices plain white bread

¼ cup whole milk

1 tsp dried oregano

1 tsp salt

½ tsp cumin

½ tsp black pepper

½ tsp paprika

For Sauce:

¾ cup ketchup

2 Tbsp brown sugar

1 tsp white vinegar

1 tsp garlic powder

½ tsp onion powder

¼ tsp salt

¼ tsp black pepper

Line a 9x5 loaf pan with parchment paper and preheat oven to 375°F. Moisten bread slices with water and squeeze into a tight ball. Chop bread finely with a knife and combine with beef in a large mixing bowl. Let bread and meat rest together for 10 minutes, then add all remaining ingredients for meat and mix well with hands.

Press meat firmly into the pan and flatten the top evenly with the palm of your hand. Bake, uncovered, for 40 minutes.

In a small bowl, combine all ingredients for the sauce with a whisk. Pour sauce over top of the loaf and spread evenly. Return pan to oven and bake for 20 minutes. Let rest for 10 minutes before slicing.

Mexican Cornbread

1 ½ cups self-rising yellow cornmeal

½ cup self-rising flour

1 cup whole milk

2 large eggs

1 cup cream-style corn (cooked)

1-2 large jalapenos, finely diced (about ¼ cup)

¼ cup finely diced yellow onion

1 ½ tsp salt

pinch of chili powder

Add 1 Tbsp of bacon grease to a 10-inch cast-iron skillet and place it in a 400°F oven for 15 minutes.

In a large mixing bowl, combine all ingredients and mix thoroughly. Carefully remove the skillet from the oven and swirl grease around, making sure it coats the bottom and sides well. Pour batter into skillet and bake at 400°F on the middle rack for 15-20 minutes, or until top is a light golden-brown.

Let it cool for about 10 minutes, then invert the pan onto a large plate before slicing. Cornbread should slide out in one piece.

Chapter 3
What on God's Green Earth?

There used to be a slogan down here that read, "Cotton is King." The fertile, alluvial soil of the Delta floodplain is the proverbial foundation on which Mississippi was built. In some places, it is so rich that it isn't even brown; it's black and feels like a sponge if you squeeze it. Cotton has a very weak root system, so this soil is perfect for those roots to push through with ease in order to establish the plant. At a time when clothing manufacturers were popping up all over the world, cotton was the perfect crop. But, like all commodities, prices rise and fall. As cotton prices fell, farmers were discovering the new hybrid corn that could produce upwards of 200 bushels per acre. Soybeans were introduced soon after, and up to this day, these are kings. Our economic ladder was actually a grain elevator. We used it to get to the top, and, once up there, we looked out across our great state and, instead of marveling over our financial achievements, turned to each other and said, "Oh my God, what have we done?"

In the short span of 100 years, we supplied a lot of the world with cotton, became very wealthy, built cities, introduced new crops, got even richer, and only then realized that we had been tricked. Secretary of Agriculture Earl Butz gave his famous command during the Nixon administration to "Get big or get out," stating that in the growing global economy, the only way that American farmers were going to be able to compete on the world stage was to plow up and plant their farms fencerow to fencerow. This act would prove to decimate our rich soil due to intensive crop spacing and lack of rotation of the crops, as well as become the villain in wiping out much of the natural habitat for many species of wild animals, including my grandfather's beloved bobwhite quail.

Southerners don't regard science the way that they do history. Science told them that this was going to be a disaster, but history said that they were farmers, sharecroppers, and descendants of the hardest-working men and women the country had ever seen. So they farmed. The government began to subsidize loans for land and equipment, the farmers took the bait, and the trap was sprung. Here we are today, living in one of the most capable agricultural states in the country, with the capacity to grow enough food to supply a number of states, and our main crops are GMO corn and soybeans, which are hardly food. To top that off, we ship the majority of that overseas or convert it into items that don't even resemble food. So, what lesson came behind this detrimental act? "Go to college and earn a degree, start a career in anything but farming; the work is too hard, and there's no money in it." Generations of practical wisdom on how to grow nutritious food were lost in a hazy cloud of hogwash. College is wonderful, and having the option to choose any career path one wishes is an American birthright, but who's going to grow the food?

Before this factory farming model grew into the beast it is today, a farm was not a wide expanse of land planted with one or two crops. Each homestead had a garden and animals on the land that served as workers as well as sources of protein. The animals provided an abundance of fertilizer, mostly in the form of their manure. The soil was dark and rich after years of being there, teeming with life of beneficial bacteria and other microorganisms living in the top layers, which is what supports healthy plants. Well, it's not like that anymore. Draft animals were replaced by tractors, the price of beef dropped to the point that cattlemen had to stock more cows on less land to make ends meet (leading to over-grazing and soil erosion), and chickens have pretty much become a hobby to anyone who isn't contracted by companies to raise them by the millions in confinement houses.

Business uprooted practicality, and there was a paradigm shift in farming. A true farm is sustainable, and sustainability is only acquired by having animals and crops harmonizing together. The old methods of producing food were not based on income; they were a circumstance of a way of life for people to keep food on their tables. These folks understood back then, by their connection with nature, that all things seek balance. In a natural setting, there are always trade-offs between plants and animals or animals and other animals. Anyone today who has driven by a pasture full of cows and noticed the white egrets perched on the backs of the herbivores has witnessed this taking place. The birds devour the insects, eggs, and larvae that are found on the animals and in the waste they leave behind. These things produce harmful bacteria in the soil that can find their way onto a blade of grass the cow may ingest, which could make the cow sick. So, the cows feed the birds, and the birds keep the cows healthy.

We have come a long way from growing food in harmony with the land. Many of us have been fooled by the radical dogma preached by some of the top universities in the nation (which really blows my mind), stating that petro-based fertilizers and pesticides are the answer to all of nature's problems. Although these do serve a purpose and have earned their rightful place in agriculture, it's best that we know the difference between remedies and solutions.

Truth be told, there are no solutions to some of the problems we encounter when growing food. When we spray a pesticide to kill whatever it was that was bothering us that day, we are potentially disrupting the cycle of life that the soil depends on to keep the plants healthy. Fertilizers can weaken the cellular structure of plants if not used properly, natural fertilizers included. A weak plant sends out a chemical signal that invites pests to come in and destroy it, demanding a higher application rate of pesticide. This should explain why the chemical companies, most of which are in other countries, are getting richer, and our farmers are struggling to keep their farms.

A moth lays its eggs on a vegetable plant. That moth feeds bats, which also eat pesky mosquitoes. The moth's eggs hatch, and the caterpillars eat up a little bit of the crop. That's not really as big of a problem as it seems. Birds eat the caterpillars, along with other insects, like aphids and mites. Larger birds, such as hawks, eat the smaller birds or feed them to their young, which will grow up to hunt things like moles, tiny animals that can destroy a garden with much more efficiency than an insect could ever dream about. More rodents and less hawks equals more snakes. Who wants snakes in the garden? Not me.

So, the application of pesticides to protect your precious tomatoes has the power to throw the entire system out of balance. Not to mention the health risks involved in humans eating vegetables laced with poison or the inferior crops that suffered from lack of pollination because of all the insects that died; now Grandma won't have any bluebirds to watch while she sits on the porch and sips her sweet tea. If you can live with the death of hundreds or even thousands of God's creatures, then that's one thing. But you don't want those birds weighing on your conscience.

For many people, the idea of owning a farm is only a fantasy, requiring large capital investments and a commitment to a way of life that demands a lot of hard work for little pay. But many men and women in this country, especially in the South, are very passionate about growing plants and raising livestock. The answer to the dilemma is to scale it way down to an easily manageable piece of land and, based on age-old methods, grow food in a manner that will supply your family and offer that lifestyle that one seeks without all of the stress involved with conventional farming. The backyard garden is the perfect project for this. This is where children can learn not only about where their food comes from but also the value of hard work.

There is nothing in this world more satisfying that seeing the fruits of your own labor. To walk the rows of a garden that you carved out of the earth with your own hands in search of pesky weeds or dying plants is not only a Zen-like form of honest work, but it also gives you a personal relationship with the food you eat. Every day, you must battle the weather and prune and tie up plants that keep falling over as if they are just determined to live like slobs. And then, one day, it appears like a tiny yellow trophy that God has rewarded you with for your great stewardship: the first tomato bloom of the season. It is only the first of many to come, as the garden will soon explode into a kaleidoscope of shapes and colors. But gardening can be complicated, and only when one fully understands that Mother Nature always has the upper hand will they unlock the door to the enjoyable experience of growing food.

We are so blessed to live in a part of the country that allows us to grow some really delicious food for a very long season. At our small family farm in Terry, Mississippi (USDA zone 8a), we grow dozens of different varieties of fruits and vegetables. The first planting of carrots, beets, and sugar snap peas happens in January. As soon as April 1st, we put our first tomatoes in the ground, then immediately followed that planting with sweet corn, okra, squash, peppers, and eggplant. The second week of December marks the end of our 335-day growing season, as we will harvest the last broccoli, cabbage, and greens. All of this dead plant matter is combined with the chicken litter from our laying hens to become compost, which will be spread the following spring.

The idea is to model nature as best we can. The wide diversity of plants and the chickens, serving as gleaners and fertilizer, brings us closer to that model. We do not spray pesticides, and our only fertilizers are all-natural. The result is a superior product that offers our family and friends some very high-quality meals, complete with all of the nutrients that are *supposed* to be in the food.

If you don't have your own garden at home, then there's no need to worry. The local food movement is growing faster than ever, and farmers' markets and roadside stands are plentiful in most parts of the country. Seek them out. There is a huge difference between food that was grown in healthy soil and the stuff masquerading as food found in most supermarkets. This isn't a Ford/Chevy type of opinion; it's gospel. If you use a tomato that was grown in the middle of December in a greenhouse in Idaho to make one of the following dishes, your kids are going to feed it to the dog while you aren't looking. Fluffy will then commence licking his own rear-end to get the horrible taste out of his mouth from the abomination you have created. I will accept no criticism for this. I told you so.

Pork is a Vegetable

Pork is an essential ingredient used in; I think it would be safe to say, at least half of the dishes served at the supper table. I'm not just talking about ham, lean, or center-cut chops but all of the not-so-glorious pieces as well. Rooter to the tooter. Hocks, jowls, and feet, just to name a few, should always be added to a pot of beans or greens. If the idea of a hog's foot simmering in your pot of Crowder peas offends you, then you can substitute for a ham shank or something of that nature. The fact of the matter is this is how you make food taste good. If lemon complements fish well, which it surely does, then it is easy for us to understand pairing flavors like this.

Adding lots of meat to side dishes shows a complete lack of respect for the virtues of the food you are cooking. So unless you want to make it into a stew of some sort and serve it as the main course, don't do that. The idea is to use a small amount of cured or smoked pork as a seasoning, just as you would with herbs and spices. If you are a vegetarian, then I won't discriminate against your bland, boring pot of legumes that always seem to turn out runny to add to a long list of character flaws you brought upon them by not adding animal fat. If your religious beliefs prohibit you from eating pork, then smoked turkey wings or neck bones make a mediocre substitute.

If you prefer bacon, it's really simple to make your own. By curing and smoking your very own pork belly, you can cut it into larger chunks, then freeze them separately and use them in your recipes when needed. It's much better than the strips you buy at the store. This is how you do it:

Homemade Bacon

1 (3-4lb) pork belly, skin removed

½ cup kosher salt

¼ cup coarse-ground black pepper

1 ½ tsp pink curing salt

Combine all dry ingredients and rub all over the pork belly, working well with your fingers. Place meat in a large bag or a container with a lid and refrigerate for 7 days, flipping every day.

After 7 days, rinse with cold water. Cook a small piece in a skillet to taste. If it is too salty, soak in cold water for 30 minutes. Dry well with paper towels and refrigerate overnight, uncovered.

Smoke over your choice of wood for 3 ½ hours at 225°F. Let the meat rest for 1 hour, then wrap it tightly with plastic wrap and refrigerate it overnight. You now have a slab of bacon to cut however you like.

Stewed Purple-Hull Peas and Okra

4 cups fresh pinkeye purple-hull peas

1 cup fresh okra, cut into 1-inch pieces

¾ cup diced yellow onion

1 smoked ham hock

½ tsp white pepper

Salt

In a medium pot, add the ham hock and enough water just to cover. Cook over medium heat with a lid for 1 hour.

Add peas, onion, okra, and just enough water to cover by 2 inches. Add white pepper and simmer peas, uncovered, for 30 minutes. Raise heat slightly and continue to cook for another 10-15 minutes, or until broth thickens and peas are done but not mushy. Add salt to taste and serve hot.

Squash Casserole

8-10 small yellow squash, chopped (about 4 cups)

½ cup whole milk

2 large eggs

1 yellow onion, diced

1 green bell pepper, diced

½ cup crushed Ritz crackers

¾ cup shredded cheddar cheese, plus ¼ cup for topping

1 tsp sugar

1 tsp salt

½ tsp black pepper

¼ cup unseasoned bread crumbs

Butter

Boil squash and onion in just enough water to cover until tender. Drain and mash. Beat eggs with milk and add to the crushed crackers, along with ¾ cup shredded cheddar. Add this mixture to the mashed squash and onion, along with salt, pepper, and sugar, and mix well.

Butter a 9x13-inch casserole dish on the sides and bottom. Pour the squash mixture into the dish and smooth the top out flat so that it will brown evenly. Sprinkle the top with bread crumbs and ¼ cup of shredded cheddar, dot with butter, and bake at 350°F for 1 hour.

Zucchini Casserole

6-8 small zucchini, cubed (about 4 cups)

½ large red onion, thinly sliced

½ cup diced country ham

¾ cup cubed mozzarella cheese

½ tsp crushed red pepper

1 tsp fresh, finely chopped rosemary

2 cloves garlic, minced

½ cup Italian bread crumbs

2 Tbsp olive oil

Salt and pepper

In a skillet over medium heat, sauté the onion and garlic in olive oil until onions begin to soften, about 3 minutes. Stir in ham and cook for another 3 minutes, until the ham is lightly browned.

Mix all ingredients except bread crumbs into a large mixing bowl and toss to combine, adding a dash of salt and pepper if you wish. Transfer this mixture to a lightly buttered 9x13 inch casserole dish and sprinkle the bread crumbs on top. Bake uncovered at 350°F until the bread crumbs are browned and the casserole is bubbling around its edges, 45-50 minutes.

Orange-Glazed Carrots

1 ½ lbs fresh carrots, sliced ¼ inch thick (about 3 cups)

¼ cup light brown sugar

1 Tbsp butter

½ cup orange marmalade

1 Tbsp apple cider vinegar

Salt and pepper

Boil carrots in just enough water to cover until tender. Pour off all but ¾ cup of water. Add brown sugar, butter, marmalade, and apple cider vinegar and boil for about 5 minutes, stirring frequently. Salt and pepper to taste.

Succotash

1 small white onion, diced

1 red bell pepper, diced

1 small zucchini, chopped

2 cups fresh baby lima beans

1 ½ cups fresh sweet corn kernels

1 clove garlic, minced

1 Tbsp fresh chopped parsley

1 Tbsp butter

1 Tbsp lemon juice

¼ tsp cayenne pepper

Salt and pepper

Heat 1 Tbsp of butter in a large skillet over medium heat. Add onion and bell pepper and sauté for about 3 minutes, until onion begins to soften. Add garlic and zucchini and cook another 5 minutes. Transfer to a bowl, but do not clean the skillet.

In a boiler, add baby limas and just enough water to cover by 1 inch. Bring pot to a boil, then reduce to a simmer and cook for 20 minutes. The lima beans will turn a vibrant green. Add sweet corn and continue to simmer for another 15 minutes. When beans are soft but not mushy, they are done. Drain well and add all ingredients back to the skillet.

Return skillet to stove over medium heat and cook for 6-8 minutes. Salt and pepper to taste.

Fried Green Tomatoes

4 medium green tomatoes, sliced ¼ inch thick

1 ½ cups vegetable oil

1 ½ cups all-purpose flour, plus 1 Tbsp

1 ½ cups yellow cornmeal

1 ½ cups buttermilk

2 large eggs, beaten

1 tsp salt

1 tsp black pepper

½ tsp cayenne pepper

In a large mixing bowl, whisk together buttermilk, eggs, and 1 Tbsp flour. Add tomatoes and toss well, being sure to coat all sides. Place in refrigerator, covered, for 2 hours.

In a mixing bowl, whisk together 1 ½ cups flour with cornmeal, salt, black pepper, and cayenne pepper. Add oil to a large skillet and place over medium heat. When the oil is ready, shake the excess buttermilk mixture off of the tomato slices and dredge in the flour mixture. Fry for 2-3 minutes on each side, being sure not to crowd the skillet until golden brown. Drain on paper towels and serve with Remoulade sauce.

*Use this same recipe to fry okra. It will make 3 cups of fresh okra.

Turnip Greens

1 ½ lbs turnip greens, stems removed and rinsed well

1 small turnip root, peeled and diced

½ yellow onion, diced

2 qts water

6oz fatback

3 Tbsp bacon grease

2 Tbsp apple cider vinegar

1 small dried cayenne pepper or 1 tsp red pepper flakes

Salt and pepper

Wash greens in cold salted water well to remove any grit. In a large pot over medium heat, add all ingredients. Cover with a lid and simmer for 2 hours. Add salt and pepper to taste.

Collard Greens

1 ½ lbs collards, stems removed and rinsed well

6 slices of good bacon, chopped

1 white onion, chopped

2 cups chicken stock

3 Tbsp apple cider vinegar

Salt and pepper

Fry bacon in a large skillet on the stove until it begins to get crispy. Pour off all but about 2 Tbsp of bacon grease. Add onion and cook together with bacon until it begins to soften some.

Add collards and cook until they have wilted. Pour in vinegar to deglaze the pan and stir well before adding chicken stock. Simmer for 1 hour, covered. Add a little salt and pepper if desired.

*You can cook the collards longer if you would like them to be a little softer. You may need to add a little more chicken stock.

Stewed Cabbage

1 large head green cabbage, cored with outer layer removed

½ stick unsalted butter

1 Tbsp salt

1 tsp black pepper

1 cup water

3 strips of good bacon

Chop cabbage into rough pieces and set aside.

In a large skillet, fry bacon over medium heat until slightly crispy. Remove bacon and chop it into 1-inch pieces, reserving grease in a skillet. Add cabbage, butter, salt, and pepper to skillet and fry until cabbage cooks down some, about 10 minutes.

Pour in 1 cup of water and add bacon. Cover with a lid and cook until cabbage is very tender but not mushy, about 25 minutes.

Garlic Roasted Vegetables with Lemon and Herbs

3 cups cubed potatoes

2 cups baby carrots

2 cups cubed butternut squash

2 red onions, quartered

1 bulb garlic, halved

2 lemons, halved

1 Tbsp salt

1 tsp black pepper

1 tsp sugar

1 Tbsp fresh chopped rosemary

1 Tbsp fresh chopped thyme

3 Tbsp olive oil

Toss carrots, potatoes, onions, and butternut squash in olive oil and herbs. Transfer to a large roasting pan and toss with salt, pepper, and sugar. Toss in lemons, cover the pan with aluminum foil, and poke a few holes for steam to escape.

Roast at 450°F for 50 minutes. Remove foil, stir vegetables, and cook for another 20 minutes.

Fiesta Corn

2 Tbsp butter

½ large red onion, diced

2 jalapeno peppers, seeded and chopped

3 Roma tomatoes, seeded and chopped

4 cups fresh sweet corn kernels

¼ cup diced green bell pepper

1 Tbsp fresh chopped cilantro

1 tsp salt

Juice of 1 lime

In a large skillet over medium heat, sauté onion and peppers in 2 Tbsp butter until onions soften some. Add corn and tomatoes and mix well. Cover with a lid and cook for 10-12 minutes. Add salt, lime juice, and cilantro. Serve hot.

Creamed Corn

6-8 ears fresh sweet corn, cut and scraped (about 4 cups)

1 cup half-and-half

½ stick butter

1 Tbsp all-purpose flour

2 tsp sugar

3 Tbsp bacon grease

Salt and pepper

In a large skillet, melt bacon grease and add corn. Cook over med-high heat, stirring occasionally, until corn has started to steam.

In a mixing bowl, combine half-and-half flour and sugar with a whisk. Add to skillet and reduce heat to low-med. Cook for about 15 minutes, stirring well, until the corn has thickened and the liquid has been reduced. Add butter, then salt and pepper to taste.

*This dish really pops when you tip the pepper shaker too far.

Skillet Squash

8-10 small yellow squash, sliced ¼ inch thick (about 6 cups)

1 small yellow onion, sliced thin

1 stick unsalted butter, melted

3 Tbsp bacon grease

Salt and pepper

Boil squash and onions together in just enough water to cover until tender. Drain all but about ¼ cup of water, then add bacon grease and butter. Cook over medium heat for about 10 minutes. Add salt and pepper to taste.

Pinto Beans

1lb dried pinto beans, picked through to remove any trash

1 medium white onion, chopped

½ green bell pepper, chopped

1 small jalapeno pepper, diced

2 whole cloves garlic, crushed

1 ham hock or other meat for seasoning

1 tsp ground cumin

½ tsp dried oregano

Salt and pepper

Soak beans in cold water for at least 12 hours. Pick out any beans that float to the top and discard them. Rinse beans well and add to a medium pot. Add enough clean water to cover the top of the beans by about 2 inches. Bring to a boil over med-high heat, then reduce to a low simmer.

Add onion, bell pepper, ham hock, and garlic, then cover with a lid. Cook at a low simmer, stirring occasionally, for 1 ½ hours or until beans are soft but not mushy. Shred meat if using, add salt and pepper, and serve.

Preserving the Harvest

After you have found yourself with an abundance of produce from the garden, you will need a way to preserve some for later use. While there are many ways to preserve food, I want to focus on water-bath canning, something that is super easy but a lot of folks are very intimidated by.

The first thing you should always start with is the freshest produce you can get your hands on. You don't want very overripe fruits or vegetables or blemished ones. Next, you want a large (18-21qt) canning pot; some clean glass jars of your choice (I prefer the wide-mouth jars); a canning rack with handles that fit inside the pot; a jar lifter (not regular tongs); a wide-mouth funnel; and some new rings and lids. Rings can actually be cleaned and sterilized, along with the jars, but lids must be new.

The science behind canning is quite simple. Food is covered in both good and bad bacteria, and both need to be minimized to keep it from spoiling. In order to do that, the food must be heated to a certain temperature and held there for a certain length of time. This heating will also destroy enzymes in the food that cause it to ripen further. To prevent any anaerobic bacteria from growing later down the road, once the jar is sealed, the pH has to be kept at or below 4.6. Bottled lemon juice has a pH of right around 2.0, and unless the recipe calls for vinegar, it is the only other acid I use, as fresh lemon juice can vary in its pH. It takes very little lemon juice to reach the desired pH, so don't worry about it altering the flavor of the food.

Salt creates a very poor environment for microbes to live in. Salt also breaks down the cellular structure of vegetables and softens them, allowing any other flavors you add to be absorbed. The iodine in table salt gives a cloudy appearance and off-flavors in canning, so use salt that was designed for the purpose of preserving food.

Once the food is in the jar, the jar must be sealed air-tight. When you put a jar of food into a pot of boiling water, two things happen: first, the food is heated to the point of destroying bacteria and enzymes, as already mentioned. As it begins to cool, once the jar is removed from the pot, the contents contract, and a vacuum is created. With any luck, you are left with a perfectly sealed jar of delicious bounty from the garden. Some foods cannot be safely preserved using the water-bath canning method; they must be pressure-canned. I don't use pressure-canners because they scare me. There are great guides to pressure-canning for the daring souls who care to work in a kitchen armed with a bomb that is full of boiling water.

Jams and jellies are created with only a handful of ingredients. The sugar and pectin work in harmony to cause the jelly to "set." When heat, sugar, and pectin are all in the pot together with an acid, such as lemon juice, a chemical reaction is created. Without each ingredient binding together as one, it would be like a bunch of negatively-charged magnets floating around inside of a jar of fruit juice. As heat is applied, the sugar and pectin try to bond together. Lemon juice neutralizes the negative charge on the pectin, allowing it to form a bond with sugar. An incredibly sticky web is then spread throughout the jar, and all water is locked into place, never to run again, hopefully. Sometimes, the contents won't turn out perfectly, but this is a skill that must be sharpened over time, a lifetime even.

Southerners are very patient people, especially when it comes to cooking. Think about slow-cooked barbecue. It takes all day to prepare the meal and about 20 minutes to eat it. One thing I cannot stress enough is the importance of not rushing the canning process. Never try to double a canning recipe. Make more batches if you want more. Expect some jars to not seal properly. This is a fairly common thing, so just use them within a few days. Jams and jellies can be stored in the refrigerator for weeks after the seal is broken, or if it never was.

Stewed Tomatoes

18 cups peeled, cored, and chopped tomatoes

8 Tbsp distilled white vinegar

2 tsp kosher salt

In a large pot, cook tomatoes over med-high heat, stirring often for 10 minutes. Crush some of the tomatoes to help release their juices. Continue cooking for 25 minutes.

In a canning pot, place 4 quart-sized jars in a rack and cover with water. Boil for 2 minutes, then turn off the heat and cover it with a lid.

Remove jars, place them on a towel upside down, and let dry for 2 minutes. Add 2 Tbsp vinegar and ½ tsp salt to each jar. Fill jars with tomatoes, leaving ½ inch of headspace in each one. Remove any air bubbles and secure lids and rings to just finger-tight.

Return jars to rack in the canning pot and boil for 1 hour. Remove jars and let cool overnight. Remove rings and check seals. Tomatoes will keep up to two years.

Louisiana Strawberry Jam

10 cups fresh strawberries, tops removed

1 cup peeled and shredded Granny Smith apple

3 ½ cups granulated sugar

2 Tbsp bottled lemon juice

Roughly chop strawberries and place in a large pot.

Place four pint-size jars in a rack in a canning pot and cover with water. Boil for 2 minutes, then turn off the heat and cover it with a lid.

Add sugar, lemon juice, and apple to a pot with strawberries. Bring to a boil over med-high heat and stir together, crushing berries a little to help release their juices. Boil fruit until mixture thickens and a candy thermometer reads 218°F, about 35 minutes.

Remove jars from pot and place on towels upside down for 2 minutes to dry. While jars are still hot, ladle jam into them, leaving ¼ inch of headspace. Remove air bubbles and wipe the rims clean. Add lids and rings and tighten to just finger-tight.

Return jars to rack in canning pot and boil for 15 minutes. Remove jars and let cool overnight. Remove rings and check seals. The jam will keep it for 1 year.

Blueberry Jelly

4 cups blueberry juice

4 ½ cups granulated sugar

2 Tbsp powdered pectin

1 Tbsp bottled lemon juice

Place four pint-size jars in a rack in a canning pot and cover with water. Boil for 2 minutes, then turn off the heat and cover it with a lid.

Combine ½ cup sugar and 2 Tbsp pectin in a small bowl. Bring blueberry juice and lemon juice to a low boil in a large pot. Add 4 cups of sugar and raise the heat to high. Whisk in sugar and pectin and boil hard for 3 minutes, skimming foam from the top with a ladle. Turn off the heat.

Remove jars from pot and place on towels upside down for 2 minutes to dry. While jars are still hot, ladle jelly into them, leaving ¼ inch of headspace. Remove air bubbles and wipe the rims clean. Add lids and rings and tighten to just finger-tight.

Return jars to rack in canning pot and boil for 15 minutes. Remove jars and let cool overnight. Remove rings and check seals. Jelly will keep for 1 year.

*When juicing fruit for jelly, never squeeze the juice out of the fruit. Squeezing will make the liquid cloudy. Just press the fruit and let the juices drain naturally with the help of gravity.

Fig Preserves

5 lbs fresh figs

7 cups sugar

2 lemons, sliced very thin and seeds removed

Wash figs and remove stems. Place figs in a non-reactive bowl or Dutch oven and pour sugar over top. Cover and let stand overnight. Do not drain.

Pour fig and sugar mixture into a pot and cook over medium heat, stirring constantly, until all sugar has dissolved about 15-20 minutes.

Reduce heat to low, add all lemon slices, cover with lid, and simmer for 30 minutes. Remove the lid and stir well. Continue simmering and stirring for about 1 ½ hours or until the mixture has thickened. Attach a candy thermometer to the side of the pot and continue cooking until it reads 200°F, about 30 minutes more. Remove the pot from heat and cover with a lid.

Place four pint-size jars in a canning pot and cover with water. Boil for 2 minutes, then turn off the heat and remove jars. Place jars on towels upside down for 2 minutes to dry. While jars are still hot, ladle preserves into them, leaving ¼ inch of headspace. Remove air bubbles and wipe the rims clean. Add lids and rings and tighten to just finger-tight.

Return jars to rack in canning pot and boil for 10 minutes. Remove jars and let cool overnight. Remove rings and check seals. Preserves will be kept for at least 1 year.

A May-Who?

The mayhaw fruit, a by-product of a beautiful variety of hawthorn, can be found growing wild throughout much of the South. Usually, the trees are not cultivated due to their abundance in the wild swamps and river bottoms, but some are planted around homesteads. Mayhaw gathering is a recreational activity that occurs in the spring, which consists of tools such as johnboats, 4-wheelers, buckets, tarps, and nets. You can find them floating on the surface of river backwaters, having fallen from the trees lining the banks. Just scoop those up with a net. Sometimes, they are found in clusters of five or more, a little deeper in the woods, requiring a little more effort to harvest but no less fun. Just lay out the tarp around the base of the tree and vote on which crazy person is going to climb up it and shake the fruit free from its branches. After all the fruit has been shaken free, gather up the tarp by its corners and pour the mayhaws into a bucket.

Some nurseries carry a few varieties of mayhaw if you would like to plant some for yourself. Grow them the same way you would almost any fruit tree, such as a plum. The fun of harvesting wild fruit should not be understated, but the real reward is in the bounty itself. If you have never had fresh-made mayhaw jelly, then I highly recommend sourcing some in any way possible. If you have access to fresh or frozen mayhaw fruit, then I will be honored to teach you how to create a food item that has become a legend and is very hard to find.

Mayhaw Jelly

3lbs fully ripe mayhaw

4 ½ cups water

5 cups sugar

½ Tbsp butter

1 box powdered pectin

1 Tbsp bottled lemon juice

Place four pint-size jars in a rack in a canning pot and cover with water. Boil for 2 minutes, then turn off the heat and cover it with a lid.

Remove stems from mayhaws and place them in a large pot. Add water and bring to a boil. Reduce heat to low, cover, and simmer for about 15 minutes. Crush fruit with a potato masher and strain juice through cheesecloth until very clean. Measure exactly 4 cups of juice and pour into an 8-quart saucepot.

Add 4 cups of sugar to the pot and stir pectin into the remaining 1 cup. Bring to a low boil. Mix sugar and pectin well and pour into the boiling pot. Add lemon juice and butter and bring to a rolling boil on high heat, whisking constantly to reduce foam. Boil hard for exactly 1 minute and remove from heat. Skim any foam off the top with a spoon.

Remove jars from pot and place on towels upside down for 2 minutes to dry. While jars are still hot, ladle jelly into them, leaving ¼ inch of headspace. Remove air bubbles and wipe the rims clean. Add lids and rings and tighten to just finger-tight.

Return jars to rack in canning pot and boil for 15 minutes. Remove jars and let cool overnight. Remove rings and check seals. Jelly will keep for 1 year.

Bread and Butter Pickles

2lbs pickling cucumbers, sliced ¼ inch thick

2 medium white onions, sliced thin

2 red bell peppers, seeded and sliced thin

2 ½ Tbsp Morton Canning and Pickling Salt (do not substitute)

3 cups sugar

4 cups apple cider vinegar

1 ½ cups water

1 ½ Tbsp celery seeds

1 ½ Tbsp mustard seeds

1 ½ tsp ground turmeric

1 tsp ground ginger

In a large bowl, toss cucumbers, onions, bell peppers, and salt. Cover with ice and let sit for 3 hours. Drain in a colander, but do not rinse.

Place 6 pint-size jars in a rack in a canning pot and cover with water. Boil for 2 minutes. Turn off the heat and cover with a lid.

In a large pot over med-high heat, bring vinegar, water, sugar, celery seeds, mustard seeds, turmeric, and ginger to a boil. As soon as the mixture boils, remove from heat and cover.

Remove jars from pot, drain water, and place upside down on towels for 2 minutes to dry. Pack jars tightly with cucumber mixture.

Return the vinegar mixture to a boil. Ladle mixture into jars with cucumbers, leaving ½ inch of headspace. Be sure to divide the spices evenly.

Wipe the rims of jars clean, add lids, and screw on rings to just finger-tight. Place jars in a rack in a canning pot and bring to a boil. As soon as the water begins to boil, start lowering the heat until just below a simmer. A thermometer would read between 185°F-190°F. When this temperature is reached, set a timer for 35 minutes.

Remove jars and let cool overnight. Remove rings and check seals. Pickles will keep for 2 years.

Chapter 4
Supper Time:

Since birth, I have been surrounded by wonderful cooks, gardeners, and teachers. Daddy used to carry me out into the garden when I was very young and show me how to determine when crops were ready for harvest: corn silks turn brown, watermelons sound hollow when you thump them, and okra every 4 hours. But my favorite was the pinkeye purple-hull peas. We would fill a 5-gallon bucket up to the rim and then carry them inside, and the whole family would gather around and shell them. Before the heat from the summer sun had a chance to escape them, they would be simmering in a pot with a ham hock and a few snaps or cut okra. Later in the evening, those peas would be served to the ones who shelled them alongside something like fried pork chops, with some fresh squash and a hot piece of buttered cornbread.

Nana taught Momma how to cook, and Grandma Turner taught Daddy how to cook, so both were highly skilled in preparing meals from things grown out back in the yard. The table was where we kids would do our homework, Daddy would do his logbook, and where we would all gather for our final meal of the day. There was no going into the living room and eating in front of the television. From what I remember, it was turned off so that there was no distraction while we all sat and talked about our day. There were strict rules at the table, too: you couldn't wear a hat, couldn't put your elbows on the table, had to sit up straight in the chair, couldn't eat with your hands, and always had to give thanks to the Lord first. After we were done eating, each person rinsed his or her own plate and put it in the dishwasher. Momma and my little sister would tidy up the kitchen, my older brother and I would go watch Nick at Night, and Daddy would go out in the garage to work on his truck or straighten up his tools.

I remember one year Daddy bought Momma a Crockpot for Christmas. She had just recently become a registered nurse, and her new work hours didn't always allow time to cook a big meal in the evening. She would throw a beef roast in it with some potatoes, onions, and carrots, top that with a packet of French Onion Soup Mix, and, by the time we were all home from work and school, it would be ready to eat. All someone had to do was cook the rice. So we started eating a lot of stews and other things that could be made in the slow cooker because Daddy knew what he was doing that Christmas.

Momma knew that her present wasn't like when a man buys a woman a fishing rod so he can take her out in the boat once, and then it becomes his. She knew that he was out on the road all the time, and she would be in charge of feeding the kids and keeping the house until he got home. Daddy was a no-nonsense man and ruled over the household, but when he wasn't there, Momma did. He could be as mean as a snake sometimes, but never to her. It was just the way a lot of men were then. Men demand respect, and women need love and affection. When a man truly loves a woman, it's a soft love that makes people teary-eyed. But when that woman loves him back, it's a love that rumbles inside of her like a volcano waiting to erupt. Think about when your child or children were born; that's the way Daddy loved Momma. Now think about the love you had for your grandfather; that's how Momma loved Daddy. It was strong, Biblical, selfless love between those two, and I got to watch it grow each night at the supper table.

And that's what supper is: the place where family bonds are established, and children are hand-molded by their parents into what kind of people they will later become. Of course, food is served, but it's not about the food. There's this age-old dilemma about which meal of the day is which. Some call it the mid-day meal lunch; some say it's dinner. I've even heard it called lunch and supper by the same person. Supper is the meal that is served to people where they sit down with their family or friends, or both, and they all eat and reflect on their day. It's where people teach each other how to love better and stronger. Supper is a deadline for all things involving work and play; it marks the end of a day. No person has ever called their wife or husband and said to them, "Honey, I won't be home in time for the news." Children are instructed to be home in time for supper. Although the child may think that having to leave their friends to go in for the evening was the metaphorical equivalent of the sound of trumpets, blowing to signal the end of the world as they know it, what was worse was being late for supper and disrespecting their mother. Any form of disrespect towards Momma was the fastest way to earn a whuppin'.

A "whuppin'" is something that was manufactured in the South centuries ago to teach kids respect and manners. This is why a lot of grownups down here continue to say "yes sir" and "yes ma'am," even to people much younger than them. The whuppin' has that *lasting* effect. A "whippin'" was something you got when the overgrown redheaded boy down the street licked you in a fistfight. This is not to be confused with the whuppin' you received afterward from your parents, no matter who started it.

The elders planted fruit trees primarily for the harvest of their limbs to make switches. Peaches were the main crop because they needed to be pruned often due to the fact that the older limbs quit producing fruit. Contrary to popular belief, the best peaches don't come from Georgia. Georgia just has the most stubborn children. Little did I know as I was being educated on the life-cycle of deciduous trees, I was also learning how to differentiate fruit-bearing wood from weapons for my rear-end.

Grandma, Momma, and Daddy all whupped you differently. Momma used the "Staccato Method": I-thought-I-told-you-not-to-pull-your-sis-ters-hair! There's a lick at each syllable break. Grandma talked to the Lord for a few seconds between each laser-guided swing of the weapon, begging Him to exorcise the demons from the soul of her delinquent grandson. Daddy just whupped the hell right out of you.

But there's direction in this highly effective way of rearing your offspring. If the child acts up, the child gets the switch. If the lesson takes, the child will be forgiven before supper is served and possibly get to enjoy a bowl of peach cobbler for dessert. The peach tree has many uses.

The following recipes have been collected from family or friends or maybe stolen from someone along the way. Now, there is an art to stealing recipes that sometimes requires skills that aren't learned in church. But a person with any decency will never steal a closely guarded family secret, for one, and only some kind of heathen would steal a family recipe and then change it. That's starting rumors about people and not a type of behavior that I condone. I had the devil with some of the measurements because they have mostly been done by feel for so long. For some, this could be the first time they have ever been written down by anyone in my family. I hope they remind you of some of your childhood days, maybe even that old familiar sting of the lateral branch of a fruit tree. Here is your comfort food.

Hearty Beef and Vegetable Soup

2lbs beef sirloin, cut into 1-inch cubes

8 cups beef stock

3 large Russet potatoes

1 qt diced tomatoes

1 green bell pepper, chopped

1 cup chopped yellow onion

1 cup chopped celery

1 cup sliced carrots

1 cup fresh baby lima beans*

1 cup fresh purple hull or black-eyed peas*

¾ cup sweet corn kernels

¾ cup fresh sliced okra

¼ cup fresh chopped parsley

3 garlic cloves, minced

1 cup tomato sauce

1 Tbsp salt, plus 1 ½ Tbsp

½ tsp black pepper

2 Tbsp canola oil

Heat 2 Tbsp oil in a large stockpot over med-high heat. Season the beef with 1 Tbsp salt and ½ tsp black pepper and brown well.

Add bell pepper, onion, celery, carrots, and garlic to pot with beef. Cook for about 5 minutes or until onions begin to soften. Add beef stock, tomato sauce, and tomatoes. Bring to a boil, and then reduce to a low simmer. Cover with a lid and let cook for 45 minutes. After 45 minutes, add okra and let cook another 45 minutes.

Next, add potatoes, corn, lima beans, peas, and parsley. Cook at a low simmer for 45-50 minutes; add remaining salt, adjust pepper if needed, and serve in bowls.

*If using dried beans or peas, soaking them in cold water overnight will soften them enough so that the cooking times will not have to be adjusted.

Cheesy Ham and Potato Soup

2 lbs red potatoes, roughly peeled and diced

1 ½ cups diced country ham

¾ cup diced yellow onion

1 (12oz) can evaporated milk

1 stick unsalted butter

3 Tbsp all-purpose flour

6 cups water

1 cup shredded mild cheddar, plus more for serving

Salt and pepper

Melt butter in a medium pot over medium heat. Add potatoes and onion and cook until onions begin to soften. Add flour and cook another 3-4 minutes, allowing the mixture to thicken and start to brown some. Add half of the water and whisk to remove lumps. Bring to a low simmer for 15 minutes.

Add remaining water, ham, and evaporated milk. Simmer for 20 minutes, then add cheese, salt, and pepper to taste.

Serve in bowls topped with a sprinkle of shredded cheese on top.

Potatoes and Onions

2 lbs russet potatoes, cubed ½ inch

½ medium yellow onion, sliced thin

2 cloves garlic, minced

1 Tbsp cornstarch

2 Tbsp butter

3 Tbsp bacon grease

1 Tbsp fresh chopped parsley

Salt and pepper

Boil cubed potatoes for 4-6 minutes until they have just barely softened. Drain and place in a colander to dry well.

In a large skillet, cook onions in 2 Tbsp butter for 3-5 minutes, and then add garlic. Cook for another 2 minutes, then transfer the onions and garlic to a bowl and set aside. Reserve butter in skillet.

Heat bacon grease over med-high heat. Season potatoes with salt and pepper, then toss with cornstarch and add to skillet. Using the back of a spatula, or your hand if you wish, press potatoes down firmly into the skillet, being careful not to mash them much. Let potatoes fry without moving for 6-8 minutes, then flip in sections and press them back down. Repeat this process two more times every 5 minutes until the potatoes are crispy.

Stir in onions, garlic, and parsley and cook, stirring mixture together, for 3 minutes longer. Adjust salt and pepper and serve hot.

Roasted Chicken with Root Vegetables

1 whole chicken

2 cups fresh carrots, cut into chunks

2 small turnip roots, peeled and cubed

2 red onions, quartered

1lb new potatoes

1 garlic bulb, cut in half

2 sticks of unsalted butter

2 sprigs fresh rosemary

1 Tbsp fresh chopped thyme

1 Tbsp salt

1 tsp black pepper

1 tsp paprika

1 tsp lemon pepper

2 cups water

Rinse the chicken and pat it dry with paper towels. Rub 1 stick of butter all over the outside of the chicken. Season with paprika and lemon pepper and place on the rack of a large roasting pan. At the bottom of the pan, add all remaining ingredients and combine them well.

Cover and cook in a 400°F oven for 1 ½ hours. Remove the lid and cook for another 15-20 minutes. Chicken is done when it is golden brown, and legs can be pulled away easily.

Fried Pork Chops and Gravy

½ cup canola oil

(6) ½ - ¾ inch thick boneless pork chops

1 cup beef broth

½ cup heavy cream

1 Tbsp seasoned salt

1 ½ cups all-purpose flour

½ tsp garlic powder

½ tsp onion powder

½ tsp black pepper

½ tsp dried rosemary

½ stick unsalted butter

Salt

Heat oil in a large skillet over medium heat. Season pork chops on each side with seasoned salt and set aside.

In a large mixing bowl, combine flour, garlic powder, onion powder, black pepper, and rosemary and mix well. Dredge each pork chop in flour mixture, shake off excess, and place in skillet.

Fry pork chops, three at a time, on each side for about 5-7 minutes or until done. Do not over-crowd the skillet. When all pork chops are done, set them aside and prepare the gravy.

Scrape the skillet with a spatula to loosen browned bits from the bottom. Add 2 Tbsp of remaining flour directly to the hot grease and whisk in. Pour in beef stock and bring to a low boil, whisking well to combine mixture. When the gravy has formed and begins to thicken, whisk in heavy cream, a little at a time until a desired thickness has been achieved. The gravy will continue to thicken as more heat is applied. Add salt to gravy if needed.

Return chops to skillet and cover in gravy. Simmer for about 5 minutes, turning once. Serve hot.

Beef Tips with Rice and Brown Gravy

1 ½ lbs Top sirloin, cut into thin strips

1 medium white onion, sliced

1 green bell pepper, sliced

1 red bell pepper, sliced

1 tsp salt

1 tsp black pepper

½ tsp garlic powder

¼ tsp dried oregano

¾ cup milk

1/4 cup beef stock

2 Tbsp Worcestershire sauce

2 Tbsp all-purpose flour

2 Tbsp vegetable oil

In a large skillet, heat 2 Tbsp vegetable oil over medium heat. Season meat with salt, pepper, oregano, and garlic powder, then add to skillet. When the meat has slightly browned, add bell peppers and onion. Cook until the onion has softened and the meat is done. Remove beef, peppers, and onion and place in a pan or bowl with a lid, reserving pan drippings.

Deglaze skillet with ¼ cup of beef stock. In a bowl, make a slurry with 2 Tbsp flour and 2 Tbsp water, Worcestershire, and a little milk. Remove skillet from heat and whisk in slurry, making sure to get any lumps out.

Raise heat to med-high, return skillet, and bring to a low simmer, constantly whisking. Add remaining milk, and when a smooth gravy has formed, return beef, peppers, and onion to the skillet. Remove from heat and stir. Let it stand in a skillet for a few minutes, then serve it over white rice.

Momma's Chicken and Dumplings

1 whole fryer chicken

1 stick unsalted butter

1 (10.5 oz) can cream of chicken soup

1 (10.5oz) can cream of celery soup

1 cup milk

1 (12oz) can evaporated milk

10 flour tortillas

1 ½ tsp salt

1 tsp black pepper

In a 6qt stockpot, cover the chicken by 1 inch with water and simmer for 1 hour. Remove chicken and set aside to cool. Add all ingredients except tortillas to the pot and continue to simmer. Debone chicken and discard bones. Add meat to pot and simmer on low heat for 30 minutes.

Tear tortillas into small pieces and add to the pot, stirring after every 2 tortillas to prevent sticking. After all tortillas have been added, cook for 20 minutes at a very low simmer. Adjust salt and pepper if needed.

Daddy's Chicken Pot Pie

1 (3-4lb) whole fryer chicken

5 cups water

1 cup diced carrots

1 cup English peas

1 cup diced potatoes

½ cup diced onion

7 boiled eggs

½ stick butter

1 Tbsp salt

1 Tbsp black pepper

1 (10.5oz) can cream of chicken soup

1 cup all-purpose flour

2 Pie Dough recipe * (see final chapter)

In a stockpot over medium-high heat, add 5 cups water and chicken. Let the chicken boil for 35-40 minutes or until it is done. Reserve 2 cups of broth.

In a medium pot, sauté onions in ½ stick of butter until onions turn soft. Add 1 cup of flour and stir in until flour balls up. Slowly pour in chicken broth and stir until it makes a thick sauce. Add potatoes, carrots, and peas, and cook 5 minutes.

De-bone chicken and chop all meat together. Add meat and chicken cream to the broth mixture and combine well.

Preheat oven to 350°F. Butter a 10-inch cast-iron skillet and roll out a thin pie dough to cover the bottom. Pour in the mixture, slice boiled eggs, and lay on top. Roll out the second pie dough to cover, making sure it goes all the way to the edges. Poke a few holes for steam to escape and bake for 1 hour.

Cindy Richards' Crock-Pot Mac and Cheese

1 lb elbow macaroni, cooked and drained

1 stick butter

3 eggs, beaten

1 (12oz) can evaporated milk

1 can condensed cheddar soup

1 cup whole milk

4 cups grated red rind cheddar cheese

1 tsp paprika

½ tsp salt

½ tsp black pepper

Combine all ingredients, except ½ cup grated cheese and paprika, in a crock pot. Cover and cook on low for 4 hours. Top with leftover cheese and paprika, and cook for 15 more minutes.

Chicken-fried steak with White Gravy

2 lbs top sirloin, cut into 5 pieces

3 eggs

1 cup whole milk

½ cup canola oil

3 Tbsp bacon grease

1 Tbsp salt

½ tsp black pepper

½ tsp onion powder

¼ tsp garlic powder

1 ½ cup self-rising flour, plus 4 Tbsp

For Gravy:

3 Tbsp butter

2 cups whole milk

Salt and pepper

Tenderize all 5 pieces of beef with a meat mallet to ½ inch thick.

In a mixing bowl, combine 1 ½ cup flour, 1 Tbsp salt, ½ tsp black pepper, ½ tsp onion powder, and ¼ tsp garlic powder and mix well. In a separate bowl, beat eggs and 1 cup of milk together.

Heat ½ cup canola oil and 3 Tbsp bacon grease in a large cast-iron skillet over medium heat.

Dredge meat in flour, then egg wash, and then back in flour, shaking off excess.

Cook steaks in small batches until nicely browned on each side and done in the center, 4-5 minutes per side.

Melt butter in a pan with drippings, scraping browned pieces from the bottom. Mix 4 Tbsp of flour with a little milk to make a thin slurry. Remove pan from heat and whisk in.

Return to medium heat and slowly start whisking in milk as the gravy thickens. If it gets too thin, the heat may save you and thicken it up. Add salt and plenty of black pepper.

Grilled Pork Chops with Jezebel Sauce

5 bone-in pork chops, cut 3/4 -1 inch thick

2 Tbsp salt

1 Tbsp black pepper

1 tsp garlic powder

1 tsp smoked paprika

1 tsp dried rosemary

2 Tbsp olive oil

Combine salt, pepper, garlic powder, onion powder, paprika, rosemary, and olive oil in a small bowl. Mix thoroughly and rub mixture over pork chops, coating well. Cover and refrigerate overnight.

Grill pork chops over a hot fire on one side for about 8 minutes, then flip. Finish cooking to medium-well or until a meat thermometer reads 145°F.

*An old trick here is to take your index fingertip and press it to your thumb tip on the same hand, making the "okay" sign. With your other hand, press on your palm at the base of the thumb. That is what "rare" feels like if you were to press on the meat in the middle of the pork chop. Switch to your middle fingertip, pressing it to your thumb tip; that would be "medium." The ring finger is "medium-well," and pinky is what meat feels like when it is "well-done." A preference for many is beef at the index or middle finger and pork at the ring or pinky.

For Jezebel Sauce:

½ cup pineapple preserves

½ cup apple jelly

1 Tbsp prepared horseradish

1 tsp Dijon mustard

¼ tsp cracked black pepper

Mix all ingredients well and serve alongside pork chops.

Crockpot Pot Roast

3-4 lb beef chuck roast, fat trimmed

2 lbs red potatoes, cut into chunks

1 large yellow onion, chopped

3 large carrots, cut into chunks

2 cloves garlic, minced

1 cup beef stock

1 (10.5 oz) can cream of mushroom soup

1 pkt French Onion Soup mix

1 tsp salt

1 tsp black pepper

1 tsp garlic powder

1 tsp dried parsley

4 Tbsp all-purpose flour

¼ cup canola oil

Season roast with salt, pepper, and garlic powder. Add ¼ cup of oil to a large skillet and heat until oil is shimmering over med-high heat. Coat roast with 4 Tbsp of flour and brown well on all sides. Set roast aside.

In a large Crockpot, add about half of the vegetables, along with cream of mushroom. Lay roast on top of vegetables and add all remaining ingredients. Cover with a lid and cook on high heat for 8-9 hours without removing the lid or until the roast shreds easily. Skim fat from the top and serve.

Chapter 5

The Gulf Coast:

The Gulf of Mexico is what breathes life into the Deep South. From January through December, thousands of different types of aquatic species' congregate in tidal creeks, marshes, and barrier islands from Texas to Florida. Many more call the deep blue waters offshore home, and can be found hundreds of miles out, in water a mile or more deep. That blue water sings a song that only certain people can hear, and those people are forever touched by it and fascinated by the beauty of the sea. It sang to me and, right on cue, as if I was pointed at by a choir director, I sang back.

In the spring of 2006 I went down to visit some friends who were in the process of rebuilding their home that Hurricane Katrina destroyed the previous summer. The small town of Pass Christian, Mississippi is one of my favorite places in this world. It's a quiet little place with a big personality that defines a beach-town, with people of all different colors, cultures, world-views, and social classes. Seeing them all come together as one big family, bringing each other food, building supplies, and good company in the aftermath of a storm that, just a few months ago, had turned the only world they knew upside down, made me understand what "community" means. Communities thrive because of their resiliency, not economy alone.

One of the great men I've known, Mr. Tommy Vice, used to have a beautiful pearl white Lincoln Town Car. We used to drive over from Pass Christian into Biloxi to play poker at the casinos, and Tommy, a man of very high class, would pour us a little snifter of bourbon for the ride. You can dim the interior lights in those cars, and it gives the ambience of an old speakeasy lounge. We would ride east on U.S. 90 and sip our drinks while listening to Al Green serenade us with "Love and Happiness." Most times we would never make it to the casino, but just pull the car over in one of the harbors that line the Mississippi Gulf Coast and stare out at the stars on the water. Tommy is a romantic, a great Southerner, and a big reason why I grew up to love things that a lot of people don't. He showed me how to see those things.

One night I drove down to the beach to watch the sun set off towards New Orleans. As the sun went down I saw a sky I had never seen before. It looked as if a graffiti artist got carried away with oil-based pastels and, just as he finished his masterpiece, spilled a glass of water across the painting. I could almost make out words in the sterling-rimmed clouds that suggested the poetry of angels. It was perfect.

I realized that although the sun wasn't always there for me when I needed it, had burned my skin many times, and made life miserable in the months of July and August; it was also my best friend. Without it no life would exist, and even if it could still exist, it would be no fun. I had to have more of it. When I got back home I packed my handful of belongings and headed further south from my hometown of Byram, Mississippi. I tossed my anchor in Pensacola, Florida, immediately landed a job as a pool-boy and, with my first paycheck, upgraded a little of my fishing gear and changed my phone number. Every day after work I would rush down to a little spot on the Santa Rosa Sound and fish for dinner. Some days were better than others, but not once would I return home empty handed.

When shrimp are heavy in the bay at certain times of the year, you can stand on the shore and catch them all day in a cast-net. Private-owned grocery stores all around the city source local foods from farmers in the area, so the produce is always super fresh. Each day after I had caught my choice of protein, I would stop by the store and buy the fresh produce to carry home and prepare dinner. A typical day's shopping list would look something like this:

1 mango

1 pineapple

1 small habanero pepper

Shredded coconut

2 limes

1 little piece of ginger

1 bunch of cilantro

Almonds

Fresh butter

Cheap wine

Good wine

I would drive home with these ingredients, along with a few speckled trout and a couple pounds of shrimp, call the neighbors over, and we would feast on Trout Amandine and Coconut Shrimp with Caribbean Salsa. This way of prepping a meal is magical to me, and to this day, I keep very few groceries stocked at home. I like to buy them fresh when I plan to use them. The woods, the water, and the market are my happy places.

The point of me telling you about that was so that I could tell you this. There is no such thing as "fresh frozen," and the only time to eat seafood is when you've caught it yourself or bought it fresh from the boats that have. Food is indeed seasonal, but somewhere along our quest to control everything on earth, we've lost the ability to just live in sync with the seasons as they change. The reason God gave us four seasons was for us to appreciate all of the changes that come and go with them, food being one.

Oysters are best in the fall and winter when the water temperature is cooler. The heavy rains and excess fresh water from the rivers in the spring diminishes the flavor of the oyster. This goes back to the times before we farmed oysters year-round, and they were mostly harvested in the wild. It was known to everyone that you should only eat the oysters during months that end with the letter "r." The warm waters of the Gulf in the summer, combined with an abundance of nitrogen and phosphorus, dumped into her belly via Mississippi River, has a tendency to produce algae blooms that can find their way into the oyster (which acts as a filter), and potentially make us sick. Also, the summer months are when mollusks and shellfish reproduce, and oysters, being hermaphrodites, convert glycogen and gametes as needed to form their sperm and eggs. Not really as bizarre as it sounds, but still not very appetizing. Just know there are plenty of other things during the warm season to eat while you wait on these little delicacies to get ripe for pickin': like the blue crab.

The blue crabs lay their eggs in the summer months. During this time of year and into the fall you may see some that appear to be dying, or even dead, sometimes laying on a cool patch of sand or right at the water's edge. If the top shell has a noticeable gap in between it and the bottom on the back portion of the crab, or if the next to last joint of the translucent flipper has a bright orange stripe or ring on it, drop to your knees and praise God. You have just received a blessing. We call these "busters," and busters are only a short time away from wriggling out of these old shells and forming new ones. For the short time in between the molt and new shell, they will be soft-shell crabs. About two per person is what you need to prepare a wonderful meal of the greatest food the sea has to offer.

Gently pick up as many busters as you can gather and place them in a container with sea water and leave the beach immediately. The way we used to hatch the crabs was in one of those little round plastic pools that infants play in, with a cheap aerator for a fish aquarium or bait tank. We would lay them in the pool with plenty of water, put some Jimmy Buffet on, drink beer, and watch them all night. We usually just wasted the evening enjoying each other's company, because the process is pretty slow, sometimes taking days for them to fully molt. The good thing is that once they do molt, it takes a little while for them to form a new shell. The soft-shell crab should look and feel like it's made out of a very soft rubber. If you wait too long, about twelve hours after molt, it will develop a rather tough, paper-like membrane around it. If this happens you should just let it go.

Under the crab's belly you will see the gills, or "dead man's fingers." They look like little yellow-orange sponges with an elongated shape. Remove them, along with the face and the apron. A sharp knife is the only tool you need for this. When I say face, that's exactly what I mean. Cut from one side to the other, removing the front half inch of the crab. The apron is the little flap under the belly of the crab. A "V" shape indicates the crab is female, and a "T" shape will be a male. Most of the soft-shell's I have dealt with were female. And that's it! All you have to do now is cook them. You can freeze them, but why? You can buy them already frozen, but that defeats the purpose of all you just learned.

Cooking seafood is an easy but very delicate art. It is very easy to over-season, and even easier to over-cook. Attention to detail is stressed here because there is nothing worse than either of those. Proper handling of seafood, in order to keep it fresh, is of the utmost importance as well. Properly handled, seasoned, and cooked seafood should taste like a warm southern sea breeze, kissed with lemon and a whisper of salt, like a teardrop from a mermaid.

I had to learn a lesson in attention to detail the hard way one spring day. Let me take ya'll out on the boat real quick.

On April 16, 2008 me and two great friends decided we would go fishing at the Chandeleur Islands of south Mississippi, about 30 miles offshore. It had so far been a perfect weekend, and the trout bite is fire-hot in April, because this is when they spawn. We spent the night before readying the boat and organizing our gear for the trip. Another friend, Scottie, who had lived down there his entire life, told us that we were going to get a little bit of rough weather and that we probably shouldn't go. The weather report suggested calm winds but chances of scattered thunderstorms. Anyone who is familiar with our unpredictable weather can tell you to always listen to the locals, especially on the coast.

We pulled out of Long Beach Harbor at 5:30 a.m. and headed south towards our destination. By 9:30 a.m. we had 45 speckled trout on ice, 5 fat flounder (try saying that three times fast), and 3 nice redfish. The only bad part of catching that many fish that fast is that it cuts the trip short. But the storms usually start to form in the afternoon, so we decided it was a success, we had a lot of fun, and it was time to head back towards land.

On the way back to the harbor we hit a blinding storm that stretched from the west side of the Mississippi coast all the way east to Dauphin Island, south of Mobile, Alabama. We veered northwest off of our plotted course and in the direction of Cat Island, hoping to find shelter. Now traveling northwest, we had the bow of the vessel pointed directly into the headwinds of this storm, which were blowing at a constant 30-40 knots. We were traveling at around 20 knots, or 23mph. Our single engine Wellcraft fishing boat was doing alright in the 3-5 foot waves, but the ocean kind of does what it wants, and there were some occasional rogues that we kept getting hit with. But none of us were scared; we were all just focused on our task and trying to make it home. Then came two good ones; back to back.

The type of boats I grew up around, and still the ones that I am most familiar with are flat-bottomed, aluminum river boats. A good river boat is not designed with waves in mind. It is riveted together along the gunwale and cross sections to allow it to flex, and the focus is usually on the width of the boat for stability. Sea-going vessels are designed for fuel economy, storage, and their ability to handle rough water. The length of a saltwater fishing boat is in most cases more important than the width, because a short boat can drop between two waves, and that can be a sketchy situation. The deeper the water gets, the further the waves get apart.

The nose of the boat shot straight up twelve o'clock, and the aft section of the keel clipped the top of the second wave and slammed us into the trough in between the next set of waves. The depth finder read 18ft, but we hit so hard I swear I felt the bottom of the ocean. The hull split and two of us were sent sprawling across the deck. As we quickly scrambled to our feet we saw the water pouring in, and something hardly anyone would have been prepared for. The steering wheel was sheared off from the console and in the hands of our captain. Years of the corrosive salty water had rusted the hub away and the key component to operating this otherwise perfectly maintained fishing vessel had failed at the absolute worst time imaginable.

Our captain, Mr. Tommy Vice, gave up the helm to yours truly, while his son, Brad, used the big arms he had to lug around his whole life to hold the engine in place. If I were to stop the boat only for a few seconds, the water would start rushing in and the boat would try to capsize. So what we had worked out was me backing off of the throttle just enough so that Brad could hold the outboard engine in place while I throttled back up, and allow us to go about ten seconds at wide open throttle, then his arms would give out and he would have to let go. Each time we did this about 100 gallons of water would pour over the transom of the boat and lighten us up by almost 1,000lbs. When we had to slow down again the water would rush back in. As Brad rested his arms the engine would kick itself to the left and I would just let us go around in slow circles. If I were to stop completely we would instantly go down. But we were managing it well, plus making a little progress towards safety.

Tommy was flipping through every channel of the VHF radio sending our distress call, but no one ever answered. The boat was carrying the three of us with our tackle, about 400lbs of ice and fish, and about six inches of water, with more pouring in every second. We were going down, but in a controlled manner. Tommy pulled up the waypoints on the GPS of all of our fishing hot spots and realized that we were only a few miles from an artificial reef that Governor Haley Barbour pushed to have built out of the rubble that Katrina left when Poseidon decided to blow us his cataclysmic kiss. By some act of God we managed to make it there and, as the boat capsized, we slid over the side with almost all of our belongings and into the salty water.

All three of us wore flip-flops that day, which turned out to be a very big mistake. That reef was made entirely of broken concrete with jagged steel all in it, and was covered in barnacles, oyster shells, and pelican shit. Our foot thongs didn't stand a chance. We cut ourselves to pieces, and Brad banged his leg up real good on the rocks once when he slipped. Two things were burned into my mind that day, and any time I go out in a boat I remember them: Never wear open shoes, and always remember to check all of the moving parts of a boat.

I pulled my cell-phone, which was going in and out of service, out of my little waterproof box. I called Brad's mother in Pass Christian and told her where we were. About 30 minutes later a U.S. Coast Guard helicopter flew real low over us, stopped in mid-air, and then flew away. They dispatched a boat from Gulfport to rescue us, and we were taken to a hospital to be treated for our injuries. We left all of our gear, including our cooler of fish on top of the reef, and assumed it was lost forever, like the boat.

When we got back to the house that night, there was Scottie drinking a beer with his feet propped up on our cooler. All of our tackle was rinsed off and lined up neatly along the wall of the garage, and our fish had been filleted and bagged for us. He had taken his small marsh-fishing boat, christened the "Ditch Minnow," and retrieved all of our stuff, by himself. What a guy. It was the single greatest "I told you so" moment there has ever been.

The ironic part of the story is this: The same storm that wiped this area out three summers ago, and claimed the lives of thousands of people had, in a strange way, saved our lives. I was born on August 29, 1983 and Katrina hit on August 29, 2005. My birthday present was bittersweet, and quite a bit late, but one I will always be grateful for. Thank you Mr. Barbour for your dedication to this great state and the work you put into the restoration of the Gulf Coast and our marine resources.

We entered into the Mississippi Deep Sea Fishing Rodeo in July of that same year and I caught a black tip shark that weighed in at 99lbs, 11oz. Brad was reading a book that had a list of all of the state records and realized that my shark was about a pound heavier than the current all-tackle Mississippi state record. I took this information to one of the judges and it was determined that we had a new record. I was given a form to fill out and, in my overwhelming level of excitement, checked the box saying we were on a charter instead of the one I was supposed to. I was then instructed that I was to give a permit number that I didn't have. The record was deemed unofficial and that was about all that was said about it, other than we needed to keep quiet about it because it was caught illegally. I kept the hook I caught it on and that form as souvenirs. The next day I realized the mistake I had made in checking the wrong box. Charter boats need that permit but private boats don't.

September of that same year we were a few miles out at Cat Island fishing for redfish and I caught a bonnet head shark that weighed around 25lbs. A bonnet head is a smaller cousin of the hammerhead, the only difference, other than size, being its head isn't the "T" shape, but more like a spade shovel. We all thought it was really cool, and put it up a great fight on the light tackle I was using, but having no reason to keep it, we let him go. As a sort of joke, with me still being haunted by my blunder with the state record, Brad checked the record books that night. He walked into the living room with the book in his hand, walked over to the mini-bar, poured a glass of bourbon, and handed me both as I peacefully rocked in my recliner. The state record bonnet head shark, as of that day, was a whopping 12lbs. It was broken in 2019, and now stands at 15lbs, 2oz. Pay attention to the details!

Gulf Coast Fish Fry

3-4lbs fresh firm white fish fillets (speckled trout, flounder, or mullet are the main three we use on the coast)

2 cups yellow cornmeal

½ cup self-rising flour

¾ tsp cayenne pepper

Peanut oil (canola or corn oil are good if you have a peanut allergy)

Salt and pepper

Season fillets on both sides with salt and pepper. In a large mixing bowl, combine cornmeal, flour, and cayenne pepper and mix well.

Heat oil to 350°F. Dredge fish in cornmeal, shake off excess, and gently drop into hot grease. Do not batter the fish until you are ready to cook them, it will make the crust too thick and it will turn out greasy.

Fry fish for about 6-8 minutes depending on the size of the fillets, or until fish is floating and just barely sizzling. Be sure also to not over-crowd the fryer, it will also make the fish greasy. Place cooked fish in a pan lined thickly with paper towels to absorb any excess grease.

*This is a very basic fish-fry mix you can use on any type of seafood you wish to cook. I don't suggest seasoning the mixture heavily, especially with salt or pepper. Black pepper has high sugar content and will scorch the oil if cooking a large batch. Instead, salt and pepper the fish before coating it. It will stick to the filet and not get the grease all nasty and over-seasoned.

Remoulade Sauce

1 cup mayo

½ cup finely diced sweet onion

¼ cup finely diced celery

¼ cup finely chopped scallion

4 Tbsp ketchup

4 Tbsp Dijon mustard

3 cloves garlic, minced

3 Tbsp capers, minced

2 Tbsp chopped fresh parsley

2 Tbsp lemon juice

1 Tbsp grated horseradish

1 tsp smoked paprika

½ tsp salt

½ tsp white pepper

¼ tsp cayenne pepper

Dash of Tabasco

Combine all ingredients in a bowl with a tight fitting lid and refrigerate overnight. Whisk and serve alongside fried fish or other seafood.

Hushpuppies

1 ½ cups self-rising yellow cornmeal

½ cup all-purpose flour

¾ cup buttermilk

¼ cup finely chopped yellow onion

1 Tbsp finely chopped scallion

¼ cup sugar

1 tsp salt

½ tsp onion powder

½ tsp garlic powder

½ tsp black pepper

¼ tsp cayenne pepper

2 Tbsp finely chopped jalapeno peppers

In a large mixing bowl, combine all ingredients and mix well. Cover and refrigerate for at least 2 hours.

Using a tablespoon, scoop mixture and form into rough-shaped balls and drop into 350°F oil. Fry for 3-4 minutes, turning so that the hushpuppies cook evenly. Drain on paper towels and serve with fried fish.

Margarita Shrimp

1lb fresh shrimp, peeled and deveined

½ tsp chili powder

½ tsp kosher salt

½ tsp ground coriander

½ tsp dried oregano

¼ cup good tequila

1 lime

2 Tbsp olive oil

Fresh cilantro

Toss shrimp in a large mixing bowl with chili powder, coriander, oregano, and salt, making sure to coat shrimp well with seasonings.

In a very large skillet, heat olive oil over high heat until it reaches its smoking point. Add shrimp and cook while constantly moving them to keep from scorching. When shrimp are just turning pink (about 2 minutes) pour in tequila and set fire to the skillet (flambé). Let the fire go out on its own then squeeze the lime over the shrimp. Top with fresh cilantro, toss in skillet, and serve hot as an appetizer, or use in tacos.

Grilled Mahi with Caribbean Salsa

2lbs mahi fillets, cut into individual servings (about 6 pieces)

¼ cup white wine vinegar

1 tsp salt

1 tsp black pepper

For Caribbean Salsa:

1 fresh mango, peeled and chopped

½ cup fresh chopped pineapple, drained

half of a red or orange habanero pepper, chopped very fine

¼ cup diced red onion

2 Tbsp fresh chopped cilantro

1 tsp fresh minced ginger

1 tsp lime zest

2 Tbsp lime juice

Dash of salt

Combine all ingredients for salsa in a large bowl, cover tightly, and refrigerate for at least 2 hours.

Season fish evenly with salt and pepper and place on a clean grill over medium heat. Cook for about 3 minutes, then gently slide a metal spatula under the filet and give it a quarter turn, but do not flip. Brush fish with vinegar and cook for about 2 minutes, then flip. Cook until fish is done but not over-cooked.

Serve fish hot off the grill with the salsa over the top.

*You can use any firm-fleshed saltwater fish for this recipe. Try redfish, red snapper, grouper, cobia, or even mackeral

Sautéed Soft-Shell Crab

4-5 medium soft-shell crabs, cleaned and rinsed

2 cups all-purpose flour

½ stick unsalted butter

4 Tbsp extra virgin olive oil

½ cup Chardonnay

2 shallots, thinly sliced

3-4 cloves garlic, minced

¼ cup finely chopped fresh parsley

Salt and pepper

In a mixing bowl, add flour along with salt and pepper to taste. Dredge each crab in flour mixture and lay on a plate while you prepare the oil.

Heat olive oil in a large cast-iron skillet over med-high heat. Lay crabs in the skillet without crowding. You should be able to do 2 or 3 at a time. Cover skillet with a lid and cook for 3 minutes. Turn crabs and cook on other side, without lid, for another 2-3 minutes. Drain on paper towels and set aside.

Lower heat slightly and add shallot. Cook until it begins to soften. Add butter, garlic, lemon juice, and wine. Cook, stirring constantly, for 2 minutes. Stir in parsley and season to taste with salt and pepper. When sauce becomes thick, pour over crabs and serve over rice, potatoes, or even grits.

Shrimp Bisque

3 lbs medium shrimp, peeled and deveined

1 cup chopped yellow onion

½ cup chopped celery

½ cup chopped green bell pepper

¼ cup chopped green onion

3 cloves garlic, crushed

½ cup chopped fresh parsley

½ stick unsalted butter

½ cup all-purpose flour

1 Tbsp tomato paste

4 cups seafood stock

1 cup heavy cream

½ cup brandy

½ tsp salt

½ tsp cayenne pepper

In a food processor, combine the onion, celery, bell pepper, half the scallions, garlic, and parsley, and process until ground.

In a 6 quart cast-iron Dutch oven, melt the butter over medium heat. Stir in the flour to make a light roux. Stir and cook for 5 minutes, until it is a blond color. Reduce heat to low, add the ground vegetables, and cook for 10 minutes, until soft. Add the tomato paste into the vegetables; then stir in the stock. Whisk to remove any lumps, and simmer for 10 minutes.

Add shrimp, then add heavy cream, brandy, salt, and cayenne pepper. Simmer for 15 minutes. Add the remaining green onions and serve in bowls.

Chapter 6

<u>Jazzin' It Up:</u>

At age 26, I went to visit a friend in Fort Myers, Florida. Daniel Koller III, a Florida native, is one of my best friends and, when we were younger, one hell of a wingman. He arranged our "fishing trip" together to also include the best friend of his girlfriend at the time to arrive the same time as me. She's still the prettiest thing I've ever laid eyes on; a Yankee girl with one brown eye, one blue eye, and a tan (I didn't even know they had sun up there). I played my cards just right, and somehow tricked that poor thing into taking a liking to me. The four of us had a great time partying it up in southern Florida, and I cried a little when the snowbird flew back home. A month later I was driving a thousand miles through ice storms and blizzards to see her again. From Florida in December to Michigan in February is quite a jump in climate, but I'd have done it peddling a unicycle as long as she'd be there to greet me.

Sometimes things just line up right and plans come together perfectly. I guess anyone who has ever won the lottery can explain this feeling, but not to the extent that I felt it. My new lady was a rare gem, and how we met was really a long-shot chance if there ever was one. I figured it like this. There are 50 states and 330 million people in this country. The chance of 2 people being in the same state at the same time is 1 in 100, if neither one lives in that state. But because it was winter, and she was from Michigan, and the state was Florida, those odds are adjusted to 1 in 60. So a 1 in 60 chance of us meeting is reduced much farther by the odds of us being in the same city, the same street, and the same apartment where we met, even with the help from our friends. Factor in all other variables and, by my math, the odds of us meeting were 1 in 4.8 billion; about as likely as flopping a royal flush 50 times in a row in a game of Texas Hold-Em.

I finally got her to come down to Mississippi in June of that same year. The plan was to show her around the South and introduce her to some of our people. Well, my friends all scared her; I took her down in the swamp and showed her an alligator, that really scared her; she tried grits for the first time and spit them across the kitchen; we drove down the Natchez Trace and she used up three SIM cards in a digital camera in the first 10 miles; took her jugging for catfish on Ross Barnett; but the thing that she liked most about the South, other than my Momma, was New Orleans.

Before I foolishly took a job that required me to travel around the country and never come home, eventually leading to the end of mine and Miss Michigan's relationship, we spent three days in the city where we stayed in an old hotel just north of the French Quarter. We partied on Bourbon Street like we were celebrating our 21st birthdays; drinking things with names like "Water Moccasin" and "Huge Ass Beer." We ate at places with names like "Pierre Maspero's" and "Willie May's." We even walked down streets named "Corondolet" and "Esplande." But the greatest memory I have of our visit was seeing this person who, other than a vacation or two to south Florida had never been south of Ohio, navigate the city like she had lived there her whole life. That's just the way it accepts you as one of its own I guess. Anyone is welcome and anything goes.

New Orleans is different than any city I've ever been to. You can smell the food cooking as you drive down towards the river and deep into the downtown area. You can feel yourself sinking further and further below sea level because of its bowl-shape and geographical location. And just like a bowl of gumbo that you can find anywhere you look in the city; New Orleans contains ingredients from all over the world. Whether you are in the mood for an elegant meal in or around the Quarter, or something with a little zing in Tremme, this place has it all. Named "Crescent City," because of its location in a crescent-shaped bend in the Mississippi River, the Port of Orleans was founded in 1718 by Sieur de Bienville. In 1762 King Louis XV of France secretly gave New Orleans to Spain. In 1800 Spain secretly gave it back. In 1803 France sold the territory to the United States in the famous "Louisiana Purchase." In 1812 Louisiana became the 18th state of the Union with New Orleans as its capitol city. Today you can still see this French and Spanish style in the architecture, as well as the food, all throughout Louisiana.

It's easy to confuse the modern culture of New Orleans with how its residents actually live and eat. Folks in the city are still rooted in the bayous. Although a lot of them have given up the life of trapping and fishing for a living, and now have higher paying jobs, they still do both for food and sport from time to time, because it's who they are. These Creole people have been here for hundreds of years. They are a mixture of Spanish, Italian, French, African, Islanders, German, and Native American. The Cajun's, not quite as long, with most of them showing up around the middle of the 18th century, after they fled French Acadia. There is a slight difference in Creole and Cajun people and some of the food they eat, but the line is so blurred that I can only taste the difference, not really see it. Creole cooking uses a little more heat than Cajun in most dishes, but not all of them. And Cajun cooks rarely include tomatoes. I think because of the heat and low-lying land, tomatoes would have been nearly impossible to grow.

Creole food is kind of like Cajun food with the twist of the African and Haitian people. Okra, in its language of origin, is called "ngombo," and is used as a main ingredient in a lot of dishes by the people of New Orleans. The Cajun, or French Acadian cooks, introduced to the region the art of producing a roux, by mixing equal parts fat and flour and cooking it down to a thick, tar-like base for stews. The Native Americans dried and ground the roots of the sassafras trees in the area to produce the filé powder used to thicken their stews. The Creoles borrowed these tactics and, by adding their own touches, prepare now what many would argue to be the best gumbo; the one with tomatoes in it.

If you have to see all of this to decide for yourself, then get out of the city and down into the heart of this land. Just head west on I-10 until you start to see exit signs that you need a translator to read to you. Or down into the Atchafalaya River Basin to towns like Thibodaux, Morgan City, or Houma. Tell someone that you want some good food, but enunciate well, you may be hard to understand. I don't want you to get hexed by a Voodoo priest and lose your sense of taste. But if you do, the cure is a bottle of Tabasco sauce from Avery Island, which isn't too far west from where you'll be. And for a shrunken head, drive back to the Big Easy and have a Hand Grenade from the Tropical Isle. Just one though, or your head might grow too much.

You see, folks down here like to party. I'm not talking about getting all dressed up and going to a social gathering at a big, fancy house where someone is coming around with a tray of champagne while Chopín plays softly in the background. Shoot me. I'm talking back the truck up to the fire, make the ladies a drink, and crank the Hank. If it starts to rain the party moves into the shop, or the barn.

The thing about parties, whether they are inside or outside, is that the people are there to have a good time, and they want some good food. Now you can be a mediocre host and go buy a bunch of precooked food, such as pizza, or you can give your guests something that was custom-made just for them. When people go somewhere to eat, drink, and be merry, they want to feel important. They want to be treated as if they were family or royalty even. Restaurants that know this stay open longer.

There are many gatherings that fall into this category: holidays, football games, birthdays, anniversaries, baby showers, barn raisings, even funerals are a celebration of the life God has given us. You've got to find your own excuse to need to have a party.

Sometimes the party takes place out of necessity. In the old days folks would perform their hog killings once the weather turned cold in the fall. Neighbors, family, and friends would all come to assist in the cleaning and butchering, and then the pork would be cured, smoked, and put away to supply the families with food for the winter. In Louisiana this is still being done today just like it's been done for centuries. The Cajuns call this a "Boucherie." If you ever get the chance to attend one, do not miss it.

The event starts very early in the morning, as they fill big pots with water and put them on to boil. After the hog is killed and bled out, the blood, kidneys, liver, heart, stomach, and intestines are reserved for later use. The animal is then scalded with hot water and scraped clean of all hair. This is a tedious process that takes some advanced knowledge and experience. The head is removed and set aside to later be boiled with seasonings and be made into souse, or "hogshead cheese;" a jellied meat that is typically served with crackers.

With the animal cleaned, it is now ready to be butchered. The hams, shoulders, shanks, feet, loin, belly (bacon), and ribs are all trimmed accordingly, then cured or smoked. The fat is rendered down in a big iron cauldron to make lard, and the trimmings are fried into cracklins'. All of the organs will be made into various types of sausage, including boudin, and the intestines will become the casings for the sausage or be made into chitterlings. About the only things that don't get used in some way are the oink and the pig's last meal. But if you don't wash the chitterlings good, you'll be eating some of that. I don't eat chitterlings; they stink, no matter how good you clean them. But clearly nothing goes to waste here. We often joke that buzzards don't live in south Louisiana because they all starved to death.

Another traditional gathering is called a "Cochon de Lait." This translates to "pig in milk," but that ain't all it means. A suckling pig weighs about 20lbs, and isn't really big enough to feed more than about five or six adults. Typically a hog weighing around 100lbs is used here, and the party usually consists of about three whole families, the neighbors, a kid or two from down the street, a deputy sheriff who was just passing by, and the ones cooking the pig.

The animal is prepared by scalding and scraping all of the hair away, the insides are removed, then the hog is butterflied by splitting the backbone. Seasonings of garlic, cayenne, and a liberal amount of salt and black pepper are rubbed in and the hog just kind of hangs out while the pit is prepared. This cooking pit may range in size and design, but usually is just a square hole in the earth that measures about 5 feet in length, 3 feet in width, and 3 feet deep. A bed of hot coals, usually pecan or hickory wood, is kept in the bottom of the pit, with a little more on the end that the hams will be on. Cinder blocks are stacked four-high, with the second row from the ground having every block turned so that the holes are facing outwards. Three-quarter inch rebar is inserted through the holes and tied together with wire where they intersect. This is where the pig will lay in the pit, and then a piece of metal roofing will cover the top. As the pig slowly cooks throughout the day, it is continuously basted with a mixture of water, apple cider vinegar, and salt to keep the meat moist through the long cooking process. Cooking time is 70 minutes for every 10lbs.

It may be because I have relatives in Louisiana, or because I just really love the culture down there, but I am very biased when it comes to their style of Southern cuisine. The thing that I am mostly attracted to is how many of their meals are these large communal gatherings that sometimes last all day. Our love for a good party seems equal.

A crawfish boil, for example, starts in the morning, or, in a lot of cases, the day before. The fishermen run the baskets in the ditches and flooded rice fields and fill the sacks. The crawfish are then washed and the cooking starts by slicing the vegetables and other things that go in the pot. The pot usually contains lemons; onions; garlic; corn on the cob, red potatoes; mushrooms; link sausage; salt; and many spices. The crawfish are lowered into the boiling water, and this cools it tremendously. The cook watches carefully for the water to begin boiling again then, once it does, he gives it 3-4 minutes, and then cuts the heat off. The crawfish soak in the hot water for about 10 minutes and it is in all of this time that the guests tell stories, play music, and enjoy their beverages. Then the food hits the table and all is quiet. This process is repeated until the last batch is cooked.

No matter what type of party you prefer, it's all about the people, and ensuring that their expectations are met and they have been thoroughly entertained. So, as they say in Cajun Country; "Laissez les bon Temps Roulez!" Let the good times roll!

The Foundations of Creole and Cajun Cooking:

There are a few things a cook must know about the French style of food cooked in Louisiana, and the main two are stock-making and preparing the roux for most dishes. The French were very peculiar about the quality of the stock used in the stews and sauces that are essentially the essence of French cuisine. The roux, as most people know, also came from the French, and is a very basic mix of equal parts fat and flour used to not only thicken stews, but also add more complex flavors to them.

The stock you buy in the grocery store is very a basic recipe that you can use in any dish that calls for it. However, if you want a stock that offers a much deeper flavor and one that actually costs much less than the store-bought varieties, you should make your own. All you need is an 8 and a 10 quart stockpot and a stove. Most of the ingredients come from the trimmings of meat, and the produce used is relatively cheap. A vegetable stock uses many types of vegetables including the addition of leeks, tomatoes, broccoli, cauliflower, or cabbage. That list could go on and on, and there are really no right or wrong ingredients. You would cook it the same as any other light stock, maybe even allowing an extra hour or two of cook time for the stock to develop its flavors.

There are a few tricks to making a good, clean stock. Always start with fresh ingredients, because the better the ingredients are the better the stock will turn out. For a more robust and darker beef stock, try roasting the bones at 325°F for 1 hour before adding to stockpot. Never stir the stock while it's cooking or the impurities will not settle to the bottom. Always use clean cold water, and never put a lid on a stockpot.

Making a roux is a fairly easy task, but one that requires the cook to stand over it, gently stirring, for the entire time. If you leave a roux unattended while it's cooking it will most definitely burn. If your phone rings and you stop stirring just long enough to answer it and tell them you will call them back when the roux is done, the roux has burned. If you get it on yourself by accident, you will burn. They call it "Cajun Napalm," and for a very good reason.

The types of fat used in preparing a roux can vary, but the use of all-purpose flour never will. If you wanted a base for a béchamel sauce you may choose to use butter to produce your light blonde roux. If you wanted to make a heavy dark roux for a dish such as gumbo or sauce piquant, you may want to use a more stable cooking oil, such as peanut oil.

The differences in the color have to do with the thickening power of the roux. A lighter roux hasn't broken down the flour completely and it will retain a greater ability to thicken the liquid it is applied to. A dark-brown roux used in most gumbo recipes doesn't even resemble flour anymore in sight or smell. The smell will be somewhere between toasted almonds, coffee, and chocolate. And the virtues of the flour as a thickening agent will have been mostly lost. The roux now has a different function in the recipe, and that is to add a much deeper flavor. The use of okra in these dark roux-based stews is twofold, as the okra has now become the thickener, as well as another flavorful ingredient.

Another essential step in Cajun and Creole cooking, as you will see listed of more than half of the following recipes, is the use of green bell pepper, yellow onion, and celery. The French call this a mirepoix, and it traditionally has equal parts onion, carrot, and celery. The people of Louisiana have adopted their own mirepoix, and swapped the carrot for green bell pepper; a vegetable much easier to grow in the hot region. They call this combination the "Cajun Trinity," and as stated before, it goes in almost everything.

So that is what I believe to be the three foundational recipes for Cajun and Creole cooking. I hope it helps you understand a little about the good people of Louisiana and their take on French cuisine.

Chicken Stock

4 quarts clean cold water

1 whole fryer chicken (3-5lbs)

2 large yellow onions, quartered

3-4 large carrots, cut into chunks

3 stalks celery, cut into chunks

½ bunch fresh parsley

1 tsp whole black peppercorns

2 bay leaves

1 garlic clove

Remove the liver from the chicken, but nothing else. Place into stockpot. Add onions, carrots, celery, garlic, parsley, and peppercorns to stockpot and pour in water.

Turn heat to low-med and cook, uncovered, for 1 hour. Do not stir. Remove chicken and debone. Place meat into freezer-safe containers or bags to be used later.

Return chicken carcass to pot and cook for 1 ½ hours. Again, do not stir. Strain stock through a fine-mesh sieve or cheesecloth into a plastic container and cool for 30 minutes. Discard all solids.

Place stock in refrigerator for at least 3 hours, but no longer than 12 hours. Remove and skim fat off the top of the stock. The stock is now ready to be used to cook with, or you can freeze it in an airtight container for up to 3 months.

Beef Stock

6 quarts clean cold water

6lbs beef bones with some meat still attached

2 yellow onions, quartered

3-4 large carrots, cut into chunks

3 stalks celery, cut into chunks

½ bunch fresh parsley

1 tsp whole black peppercorns

2 bay leaves

4 garlic cloves

In a 10 quart stockpot, add bones, onions, carrots, celery, garlic, parsley, and peppercorns. Pour in water.

Cook over low-med heat at a very low simmer, uncovered, for 12 hours. Do not stir.

Strain through a fine-mesh sieve or cheesecloth into a plastic container and cool for 30 minutes.

Place stock in refrigerator for at least 3 hours, but no longer than 12 hours. Remove and skim fat off the top of the stock. The stock is now ready to be used to cook with, or you can freeze it in an airtight container for up to 3 months.

Seafood Stock

Before I give you this recipe I want to explain a seafood stock. A seafood stock is only used to enrich the dish with a much more complex seafood flavor. Say, for instance, you were making a seafood gumbo and instead of using a light stock, such as "vegetable" or "chicken," you wanted the deep flavors of the shrimp or fish to shine through. You would use a seafood stock. I rarely use them when preparing communal meals because some people are a little skeptical about the ingredients used in making the stock.

If you do want to make a traditional seafood stock, such as the ones used by many world renowned chefs to enrich your recipe with the deep flavors, try to seek out the freshest fish you can find. Many stock recipes say you can use freshwater fish to create them, but I say you can't. Red snapper is the only fish head I will stick in a pot in my kitchen. The rest of them seem to somehow permeate the interior walls of a house, and it takes 2-3 days to get the fish smell out. That's right, I said heads. A seafood stock can use an entire carcass of a fish, including the head. It is very delicious and it does make a much deeper flavor, but for the less adventurous types, you can make a great seafood stock with shrimp and crab shells.

4 quarts clean cold water

2lbs fish bones, heads, shrimp shells, crab shells, or a mix of all

2 yellow onions, quartered

3-4 large carrots, cut into chunks

3 stalks celery, cut into chunks

½ bunch fresh parsley

1 tsp whole black peppercorns

2 bay leaves

4 garlic cloves

1 cup Chardonnay

In an 8 quart stockpot, add shells, onions, carrots, celery, garlic, parsley, and peppercorns. Pour in water and wine.

Cook over low-med heat at a very low simmer, uncovered, for 1 ½ hours. Do not stir.

Strain through a fine-mesh sieve or cheesecloth into a plastic container and cool for 30 minutes.

Place stock in refrigerator for at least 3 hours, but no longer than 12 hours. Remove and skim fat off the top of the stock. The stock is now ready to be used to cook with, or you can freeze it in an airtight container for up to 3 months.

Blonde Roux

¾ cup melted butter

¾ cup all-purpose flour

In a large skillet, heat the butter over medium heat. When butter is sizzling, add flour and whisk in.

Reduce heat to low-med and cook, stirring constantly with a wooden spoon, for about 10 minutes.

Dark Roux

¾ cup peanut or canola oil

¾ cup all-purpose flour

In a large skillet, heat the oil over medium heat. When oil is hot and shimmering, add flour and whisk in.

Reduce heat to low-med and cook, stirring constantly with a wooden spoon, for about 30 minutes.

Chicken and Sausage Gumbo

¾ cup all-purpose flour

¾ cup canola oil

6 cups chicken stock

1lb cubed uncooked chicken meat, light and dark mixed

1lb andouille sausage

1 ½ cups chopped yellow onion

1 cup chopped green bell pepper

1 cup chopped celery

1 cup fresh cut okra

4 cloves garlic, crushed

2 tsp dried thyme

2 tsp garlic powder

2 tsp onion powder

1 tsp smoked paprika

1 tsp black pepper

1 tsp white pepper

½ tsp cayenne pepper

¼ cup fresh chopped parsley

¼ cup fresh chopped green onion

2 bay leaves

Tabasco sauce

Salt

In a large pot, make a dark roux with flour and oil. Reduce heat to med-low and add onions. Cook until roux becomes shiny and onions begin to soften.

Add 1 cup of chicken stock and stir until well combined with roux. Add sausage, celery, bell pepper, garlic, and okra. Slowly add all remaining stock, while stirring, until well combined. Bring to a low boil and add chicken, bay leaves, thyme, garlic powder, onion powder, black pepper, white pepper, and cayenne pepper. Cook for 30 minutes, skimming fat off the top with a spoon as gumbo cooks.

When chicken is done but not stringy and falling apart, add fresh herbs. Cook an additional 10 minutes, remove bay leaves, and serve over rice.

Red Beans and Rice

2 cups beef stock

1lb dried kidney beans

1lb andouille sausage, sliced into ¼ inch rounds

2 bay leaves

1 cup diced yellow onion

1 cup diced celery

1 cup diced green bell pepper

3 cloves garlic, minced

1 Tbsp brown sugar

1 tsp salt

1 tsp black pepper

½ tsp white pepper

½ tsp dried oregano

¼ cup fresh chopped parsley

¼ cup fresh sliced green onion

1 Tbsp vegetable oil

Cover beans with cold water and soak for at least 12 hours. Drain and discard water.

In a medium pot, add more water to barely cover beans and cook, uncovered, over medium heat while you prepare other ingredients.

In a large skillet, brown sausage well and set aside. Add vegetable oil to skillet and sauté onions, celery, and peppers for 3-5 minutes. Add garlic and cook for 3 minutes longer.

As beans cook and begin to soften, add sautéed vegetables to pot. As water evaporates and is absorbed by the beans as they cook, add beef stock as needed to barely keep beans covered by about 1 inch. Let simmer for 25 minutes. As beans soften, take the back of a wooden spoon and smash them against the sides of the pot. This makes the beans creamy and begins to thicken them. Add salt, pepper, brown sugar, and parsley to the pot and simmer for 10 minutes.

Add sausage to the pot and cook until beans have almost all cooked down to this creamy texture. Toss in green onion, adjust seasoning and serve hot over rice.

Dirty Rice

4 cups cooked white rice

1lb ground hot pork sausage

10-12 chicken livers, chopped

½ cup diced onion

½ cup diced celery

½ cup diced red bell pepper

2 cloves garlic, minced

1 tsp ground cumin

1 tsp dry mustard

1 tsp dried parsley

1 tsp dried thyme

1 tsp paprika

½ tsp white pepper

½ tsp black pepper

½ tsp salt

1 tsp hot sauce

In a large skillet, cook sausage until it begins to brown, breaking it up with a wooden spoon. Add chicken livers and cook all the way through, then toss in onion, celery, bell pepper, garlic, parsley, and thyme. Cook for about 10 minutes, or until vegetables have softened.

Add rice and cook for another 10 minutes over med-high heat, breaking up clumps and mixing well and you go. Mix in all remaining ingredients, turn heat down to low, cover, and cook for 5 minutes. Adjust salt and pepper if needed and serve hot.

Chicken Sauce Piquant

1 whole fryer chicken

½ cup canola oil

½ cup all-purpose flour

1 ½ cups chopped yellow onion

1 cup chopped green bell pepper

1 cup chopped celery

2 Tbsp minced garlic

2 whole peeled and diced tomatoes

1 (6oz) can tomato paste

1 Tbsp brown sugar

2 Tbsp Worcestershire sauce

2 Tbsp fresh chopped basil

1 Tbsp fresh chopped thyme

½ cup fresh chopped green onion

¼ cup fresh chopped parsley

1 tsp crushed red pepper

2 Tbsp salt

1 Tbsp black pepper

1 ½ tsp white pepper

1 Tbsp hot sauce

1 bay leaf

Boil chicken until done then remove and set aside to cool. Reserve 6 cups of chicken broth. Debone chicken and set meat aside.

In a large pot, make a dark roux with flour and canola oil. When roux has reached a chocolate brown, add onions, bell pepper, and celery. Cook 3-5 minutes then add broth, 1 cup at a time, until thoroughly combined. Bring to a low simmer then add tomatoes, garlic, tomato paste, Worcestershire sauce, red pepper, white pepper, sugar, and bay leaf. Let cook for 15 minutes, stirring frequently.

Add chicken, basil, thyme, and parsley and cook for 15 minutes. Stir in green onions, add salt, black pepper, and hot sauce. Serve over rice.

Creole Seafood Gumbo

4 cups seafood stock

½ cup all-purpose flour

½ cup canola oil

2 yellow onions, chopped

1 cup chopped green bell pepper

1 cup chopped celery

1 cup fresh cut okra

4 cloves garlic, crushed

2 Tbsp fresh chopped thyme

½ cup fresh chopped green onion

¼ cup fresh chopped parsley

1 pint tomato sauce

1 tsp gumbo filé powder

1 Tbsp sweet paprika

1 Tbsp onion powder

1 Tbsp garlic powder

2 Tbsp salt

1 tsp black pepper

1 tsp white pepper

1 tsp cayenne pepper

1lb andouille sausage

1lb medium shrimp, peeled and deveined

1lb picked crab meat

1 pint shucked oysters, undrained

3 bay leaves

Tabasco sauce

In a large pot, make a dark roux with flour and oil. Reduce heat to med-low and add onions. Cook until roux becomes shiny and onions begin to soften.

Add sausage, celery, bell pepper, garlic, and okra. Add stock a little at a time to prevent lumping. When all stock has been added and mixture is smooth, add bay leaves, green onion, thyme, tomato sauce, filé powder, salt, black pepper, white pepper, and cayenne pepper. Lower heat to a low simmer and cook for 30 minutes.

Add all remaining ingredients and bring back to a low simmer. Once the pot is simmering, cook for 10 minutes. Remove bay leaves and serve over white rice with a dash of Tabasco and more filé powder if desired.

Grillades

¼ cup canola oil

3lbs top sirloin or top round beef, cubed

2 cups chopped yellow onion

1 ½ cups chopped green bell pepper

1 cup chopped celery

2 Tbsp minced garlic

2 ½ cups beef stock

¼ cup all-purpose flour

½ cup red wine, preferably merlot

1 cup diced tomatoes

½ tsp dried rosemary

½ tsp dried thyme

½ tsp dried oregano

½ tsp dried basil

½ tsp salt

½ tsp black pepper

¼ tsp cayenne pepper

In a large mixing bowl, season beef with salt and pepper. Toss with flour, being sure to coat each piece well.

In a large cast-iron skillet, heat canola oil over medium heat. Add beef to the skillet and brown well, working in batches if needed to keep from overcrowding. When all beef is browned nicely, add all of it to the skillet.

Add onion, bell pepper, and celery to skillet and cook together with beef for about 6 minutes. Add garlic and cook until it is fragrant, about 1 minute. Add all dry seasonings and combine well.

Pour in wine to deglaze the pan, scraping with a spatula to release all browned bits stuck to the bottom. Pour in beef stock and tomatoes, reduce heat to low, cover with a lid, and simmer for 2 hours. As beef is cooking, stir about every 15 minutes to prevent scorching. Add more salt and pepper if needed and serve over white rice.

Chicken and Sausage Jambalaya

2 Tbsp bacon grease

2 cups uncooked white rice

2 cups chicken stock

1lb chicken thigh meat, roughly chopped

1lb smoked pork sausage

1 cup diced yellow onion

1 cup diced green bell pepper

1 cup diced celery

1 cup diced tomatoes

2 Tbsp tomato paste

2 Tbsp minced garlic

1 Tbsp Tabasco sauce

1 Tbsp Worcestershire sauce

1 Tbsp Cajun Seasoning

1 Tbsp smoked paprika

1 tsp ground cumin

1 tsp dried thyme

1 tsp dry mustard

½ tsp salt

½ tsp black pepper

½ tsp white pepper

½ cup chopped fresh green onion

¼ cup chopped fresh parsley

3 bay leaves

Preheat oven to 350°F. In a large oven-safe pot, heat bacon grease over medium heat on stove. Add sausage and brown well.

Add onion, bell pepper, and celery to pot and cook for 5-7 minutes, stirring frequently. Add garlic and all dry seasonings and cook for about 3 minutes. Add tomatoes and tomato paste and mix well. Add chicken stock, Tabasco, Worcestershire sauce, and bay leaves and bring to a boil.

Add rice and chicken, cover with a lid, and place in oven for 20 minutes.

Remove pot from oven and stir the mixture well. Return pot to oven and cook for 20 more minutes.

Remove pot again and stir mixture well. If rice is not done yet, return to oven for an additional 10 minutes or so.

Add parsley and green onion and mix well. Let pot stand, covered, for about 15 minutes, then fluff and serve hot.

Chicken Fricassee

2 ½ cups chicken stock

1 cup all-purpose flour, plus ¼ cup

8 bone-in chicken thighs

½ stick butter

2 cups sliced button mushrooms

¾ cup chopped shallots

½ cup chopped green bell pepper

½ cup chopped celery

2 Tbsp minced garlic

1 cup heavy cream

½ cup Chardonnay

½ tsp salt

½ tsp black pepper

½ tsp dried rosemary

¼ tsp cayenne pepper

½ cup chopped fresh parsley

½ cup chopped fresh green onion

In a large mixing bowl, combine 1 cup of flour with salt, black pepper, and cayenne pepper. Dredge each piece of chicken in flour mixture and set aside.

In a large cast-iron skillet, melt butter over medium heat. Brown each piece of chicken well for about 5 minutes per side. You may have to work in batches. Do not wipe out skillet.

Add shallot, bell pepper, and celery to skillet and cook, stirring frequently for about 6 minutes. Add garlic and cook until it is fragrant, about 1 minute. Add ¼ cup of flour and combine well with vegetables. Cook for 5 minutes, or until flour loses its raw smell.

Add the Chardonnay and stir until the mixture becomes smooth. Slowly add chicken stock, while stirring, to keep lumps from forming. Return chicken to skillet, along with mushrooms.

Turn heat to low, cover with a lid, and cook for 50 minutes.

Add heavy cream, parsley, green onions, salt, and pepper. Stir together well, return lid, and cook for an additional 10 minutes. Serve over white rice.

Barbecued Shrimp

1 ½ lbs jumbo shrimp, head-on

1 stick unsalted butter, melted

2 (12oz) dark lager beers

4 Tbsp Worcestershire sauce

1 Tbsp onion powder

1 tsp smoked paprika

¾ tsp salt

½ tsp black pepper

½ tsp white pepper

2 sprigs fresh rosemary

¼ cup fresh chopped parsley

3 cloves garlic, minced

Preheat oven to 400°F. In a casserole dish or other oven-safe pan of similar size, lay shrimp in so that they are all lying as flat as possible. Add all seasonings over top of shrimp, pour in beer, melted butter, and Worcestershire sauce.

Cover dish with foil and poke a couple of holes for steam to escape. Place in oven and cook for 25 minutes. Serve with a couple of slices of toasted French bread.

*This is a pretty basic version of this dish that can be altered to your liking. Peeling and eating the shrimp is a little messy, but the flavors are well worth the effort. You can peel and devein the shrimp before adding them, but you will be

sacrificing some of the flavor from the whole shrimp. If you choose to do so, you can also double the amount of shrimp to be added, since the head of a jumbo shrimp is roughly half of the shrimp.

Redfish Courtbouillon

½ cup vegetable oil

½ cup all-purpose flour

1 tsp salt

1 tsp black pepper

½ tsp cayenne

2 lbs redfish, cut into 6 pieces

1 cup diced yellow onion

1 cup diced celery

1 cup diced green bell pepper

6 cloves garlic, minced

2 cups diced tomatoes, drained

1 cup white wine

1 cup seafood stock

1 Tbsp Worcestershire sauce

1 tsp hot sauce

1 tsp dried thyme

½ cup chopped scallions, green parts only

½ cup chopped fresh parsley

1 lemon, cut into wedges

Cooked white rice

In a large skillet over medium heat, make a light roux with flour and oil then add onion, celery, and bell pepper. Cook, stirring frequently, for 5 minutes, then add white wine, stock, and garlic. Cook 3 minutes.

Next, add tomatoes, Worcestershire, hot sauce, salt, black pepper, cayenne pepper, and thyme. Stir all ingredients together well with a wooden spoon, then press mixture down firmly in the skillet. With the back of the spoon, make six pockets in the mixture and lay the six pieces of fish in each one. Cover with a lid and let simmer for 12-15, gently shaking the skillet occasionally to prevent sticking and burning. Do not stir mixture or the fish will break into pieces.

When fish is done, gently scoop out each piece and lay over a bed of rice, one per serving, then spoon vegetable mixture over fish. Add a Tbsp each of fresh parsley and scallions, then a squeeze of lemon over top of dish.

*You can substitute another firm fleshed fish, such as flounder or even catfish for the redfish if it is unavailable. Also, "Courtbouillon" is a funny word that some folks struggle with pronouncing. The proper way to say it is "koo-bee-yone."

Crawfish Étouffée

1 cup all-purpose flour

1 stick unsalted butter

1 cup diced yellow onion

¾ cup diced green bell pepper

½ cup diced celery

1 cup fresh chopped scallions

¼ cup fresh chopped parsley

1 Tbsp fresh chopped thyme

2 cloves garlic, minced

1 bay leaf

1 Tbsp Cajun seasoning

1 Tbsp paprika

¾ tsp cayenne pepper

6 cups seafood stock

½ cup red wine, such as Merlot

½ cup Chardonnay

1 Tbsp Worcestershire sauce

2 tsp hot sauce

1 lb cooked crawfish tails

1 tsp white pepper

1 tsp salt

In a large skillet, heat butter over medium heat until sizzling. Add onion, bell pepper, and celery and cook 5-6 minutes. Add ½ cup of the chopped scallions, along with garlic and bay leaf, and cook 3-4 more minutes.

Add Cajun seasoning, thyme, parsley, paprika, and cayenne pepper and combine well, being careful to not break up the bay leaf. Cook 3-4 minutes.

Add flour to skillet and mix until all liquid has been absorbed and flour begins to cook some. Stir in both red and white wine and mix until smooth. Slowly stir in seafood stock and mix until smooth. Let skillet come to a boil, then cover with a lid and reduce heat to a low simmer. Cook 15 minutes.

Add hot sauce, Worcestershire, and crawfish tails and cook 5-6 minutes, stirring constantly and scraping bottom of skillet. Add salt and white pepper and taste to see if seasonings need to be adjusted. Serve over white rice with remaining scallions as a garnish.

Chapter 7

The Good Ol' Boys:

Southerners have a strange natural attraction to dirt and water. A lot of us have a really strong attraction to the product of those two things mixed; mud. When Southern boys first get their driver's license, they tend to spend a lot of those first few years seeing how many mud puddles they can take their trucks through without getting stuck. It is some kind of Rite of Passage into the alpha-wolf tribe when your truck becomes the "baddest truck in town." Though the times have changed in a lot of ways, I don't believe this ever will.

When we are just small children we get introduced to things like deer camp and remote fishing holes. A lot of times the only way to get down into the hearts of these places is in a truck with plenty of ground clearance equipped with aggressive mud tires. Our fathers are, to us at the time, the only men on the planet. Along with their friends, we believe that what our fathers do is what we are supposed to do as we grow older. So when they taught us how to get out and lock the front hubs in; so that the front wheels engage, or to walk the steering wheel side to side; so the lugs on the front tires will grip the edges of the ruts and help the truck along, what they were really teaching us was how men are supposed to play in the mud.

For the time between our early teachings and becoming licensed drivers, all we dreamed about was locking in hubs and working steering wheels side to side. When the day finally came that we got to actually do it, all hell broke loose in our towns, and there wasn't a mud hole within a hundred miles that us sixteen year old boys didn't know the best way to get through. You don't usually see those kids getting into things like drugs or other forms of criminal activity because the kind of fun they are having is pure and doesn't need to be enhanced. There may be a fistfight or two, or even someone sneaking away with some of their daddy's beer, but for the most part it's just good clean fun. You can be in a group of twenty or more of these country boys and there is a guarantee that you will find one thing in common among them. They don't have a care in the world.

Teenage boys don't put too much stock into the future, and it's very hard for them to wrap their testosterone-altered minds around the importance of it. But as they grow up, they start to care about things like "what if I tear my truck up?" Eventually a large amount of that mud washes out of their bloodstreams and things like jobs, girlfriends, and bills take priority over playing with their friends. But it's never gone. They always find some reason to lock in their hubs, every now and then.

Us country boys have a special skill for finding remote places to hunt, fish, and party that are only accessible by boat, foot, or 4x4.

We tell ourselves when we discover these places that "this is it," that we have finally found the mother lode of all the deer, ducks, and fishes. It's easy to let these thoughts deceive us and to be convinced of what we simply wish to believe. The truth is that we are not the pioneer of anything, and just like the hundreds or thousands of people that discovered these places before us who thought the same thing, we soon come to the realization that the only difference between this place and any other place to pursue our adventures is this place is much harder to get to. But these are kids that we are talking about or, at best, young men who are still clinging on to their childhoods. It's my belief that males don't accept truths the same way as females. You can tell a young boy that there's no such thing as Santa, and he will look at you like you are from outer space, and then give you a list of reasons why you are wrong. When you tell a young girl the same thing she just accepts it and reconfigures her thoughts on Christmas. But at some point in the boy's life, probably around his late twenties, he starts to accept these truths for what they are, and then his roots begin to establish themselves and he finally starts to see the point of it all.

What our elders were teaching us as youngsters was a lesson that would only come in handy later in life. The truck was nothing but the vessel that carried this message, and probably the only way that our little undeveloped minds would ever understand how to navigate a dangerous or tricky situation later in life. The by-product of it all was young men who knew how to steer their own lives in multiple directions and not get bogged down. The boys usually would grow up to become blue-collar workers just like their daddy, with more ambition of living the life of a country boy rather than becoming rich. They became skilled in things mechanically, such as building houses or clearing timber. As they grew up they realized that it's wasn't about going through the mud hole anymore; you go around it when you can.

There is an importance to knowing how to do things. You don't have to be great at everything, just good at the things that will help get you through the tough times. Not everyone can afford to call a plumber or an electrician every time there is a problem at home, but you can always call a friend. After all those years of boys tearing their bicycles up trying to ramp them like the BMX guys on T.V., they learned how to fix them themselves. For years they may have pretended to know what they were doing, when really they had no clue how a washing machine works, or what makes the wheels on the bus go 'round. Well, they eventually figured it all out. Now, who is the best person to call when your car won't start and you're stranded, or you can't afford a "real" mechanic? That's right, the good ol' boys; the ones that spent all those years playing in the mud. There's a reason why God put Southerners here; it's to help people. These recipes are for the good ol' boys.

This list was kept short for a reason, and that reason is that it doesn't take much to please us. This is my 3 chord country song to my friends. Eat up boys.

Garlic and Apple Pork Sliders

1 (6-8lb) boneless pork loin

1 pt apple jelly

2 Tbsp minced garlic

1 Tbsp fresh chopped rosemary

1 ½ Tbsp salt

1 tsp black pepper

½ tsp white pepper

½ tsp garlic powder

½ tsp fennel seeds

Shredded white cheddar cheese (for topping)

Hawaiian-Style rolls

For Slaw:

2 Granny Smith apples, shredded

2 cups shredded green cabbage

½ cup thinly sliced white onion

1 jalapeno pepper, diced fine

1/3 cup mayo

½ tsp onion powder

½ tsp salt

Juice of 1 lemon

Season pork with salt, black pepper, white pepper, and garlic powder. Place meat in a Crockpot, fat side up, and turn on high heat. Thin apple jelly with a little hot water and pour over top, then spread top with minced garlic and add fennel seeds and rosemary. Place lid on slow-cooker and cook for 5-6 hours, or until meat shreds easily.

Make a slaw with apples, cabbage, onion, jalapeno, mayo, lemon juice, salt, and onion powder. Cover and place in refrigerator.

When meat is done, split rolls and place on a cookie sheet with the cut sides facing up. Sprinkle cheese over rolls and place in the oven on low broil just until the cheese has melted.

Shred pork and stir well. Use an ice cream scoop or similar sized spoon to scoop meat onto buns. Top with apple slaw.

Whole Smoked Chicken

1 whole fryer chicken, rinsed and giblets removed

1 tsp salt

½ tsp black pepper

½ tsp garlic powder

½ tsp onion powder

½ tsp smoked paprika

¼ tsp dried rosemary

¼ tsp chili powder

3 cups apple juice

2 whole peeled garlic cloves

In a small bowl, combine all dry ingredients and mix well. Pat chicken dry with paper towels and rub seasoning all over, using a little extra on the breast side.

Build a medium fire in a charcoal grill on one side, leaving the other side with no fire. Add one or two small chunks of hickory, pecan, or other hardwood directly to coals.

Place a disposable pie-tin on cold side of grill. Fill pan with apple juice and add garlic cloves. Return grill grate and add lid to allow grill to heat up for 10 minutes.

Place chicken directly over pie-tin on cold side of grill, breast-side up. Return lid with the vent directly over chicken and open vent. Let chicken cook without opening the grill for 2 hours.

When chicken is done, let rest on a platter for 5 minutes then carve and serve.

Dry-Rubbed Spareribs

1 slab pork spareribs (3 ½ - 5 lbs)

1 Tbsp brown sugar

1 ½ tsp salt

1 tsp chili powder

1 tsp onion powder

½ tsp garlic powder

½ tsp black pepper

In a small bowl, combine brown sugar, salt, chili powder, onion powder, garlic powder, and black pepper. Mix well.

Rub seasoning all over ribs, using more on the top than the underside. Let rest at room temperature while you prepare the grill.

Build a medium charcoal fire on one side of the grill, leaving the other side with no fire. When you can hold your hand 6 inches above the grate over the coals for 3-4 seconds comfortably, the fire is medium. If too hot, just let it burn down some.

Place ribs meat side up on the cold side of the grill. Cover with lid having the vent directly over the ribs, and cook for 1 ½ hours without opening lid.

Remove ribs from grill and lay on a single sheet of aluminum foil. Fold foil around the sides of the meat but leave the top open. Return to same side of the grill and replace lid. Cook 1 more hour.

Remove ribs and let stand 10 minutes, then carve and serve.

Chapter 8

Icing on the Cake:

No meal, no matter where you're from, is complete without dessert. It just so happens that where I'm from is also the home of some of the best fruit on the planet. In the summer, wild blackberries line fencerows for as far as one can see. People just park their vehicles on the side of public roads and fill buckets with the sweet fruit to take home. U-Pick blueberry and strawberry farms are found in nearly every county or parish in southern Mississippi and Louisiana. You just pick however much you want, and then the landowner charges you a small fee. Even some of the citrus trees grow quite well as far north as Tennessee. I love that; "as far north as Tennessee" (I live 3 hours south of the state-line). And if you don't think that apples grow down South because of the heat, I will tell you that Pink Lady, Gala, Fuji, and Granny Smith varieties thrive in it.

If you've never had a freshly cooked blackberry cobbler in a 100 year old cast-iron skillet, and seen the way that the berries almost liquefy and the butter fries the crust around the edges to a golden-brown perfection, then bless your heart. If you've never walked out to the henhouse and gotten your hand pecked while trying to bump an overly-protective chicken off of her eggs to use to whip up a perfect meringue for topping off a homemade banana pudding, then I pray some day you will. And if nobody has ever taught you how to properly make a pound cake by first sifting all of the dry ingredients, twice, then adding the dry to the wet, and not over-mixing, then let me be the one.

Dessert, being the capstone to the meal, requires the one preparing it to really put some heart into it. Every great cook I ever knew understood this and took great pride in carrying out each step to ensure that the people they were feeding would take one bite and make that face that has become cliché on the foodie shows on television. You know the face I'm talking about. But it's real, and every time I make my Nana's German Chocolate Cake I'm reminded of all of the strange, animal-like sounds my other family members would make when Nana baked it. Her Ambrosia Cake made them all catch the Holy Ghost. My sister can make a Blueberry Pound Cake, glazed with a thin lemon icing that is like biting into a cumulus cloud. I've seen people almost faint over this one. I had to get up from the table once and check my poor Momma's pulse.

There used to be a restaurant in McComb, Mississippi called Porches. I had some family down there that we would go visit and, because when Southerners try something they like once, it becomes tradition, we would always eat at this fine establishment that has now been closed for years. They had on their menu a Hot Pineapple Casserole, and to this day I have never tasted anything more decadent and just downright delicious. It was bound together with Ritz crackers and topped with cheddar cheese that was still bubbling when it hit the table. I was 10 years old the first time we went there and this was the thing that jumped off the menu, slapped me across the face, and demanded I order it. Now, understand that my family consists mainly of skeptics who have serious reservations when it comes to trying new foods. We didn't have a milkman, so I'm still trying to figure out how I am the only one in the family who is willing and ready, at any time, for a new experience in life. That's exactly what I found too.

After the first bite my eyes started to water a little bit. It was still a little hot from the broiler and burned the tip of my tongue, but I kept going. Second bite I got a lump in my throat. My aunt Cindy noticed I didn't look all that great and asked if I was alright. I guess her concern coaxed the rest out of me, because I erupted. I'm not talking about a few sniffles and puffy eyes. I was crying with my mouth agape, wailing, with tears pouring down my face. Momma took me into the restroom to calm me down and, because it was one of those episodes where the child can't even speak, she still didn't know what was wrong and assumed I had been burned. I finally got the words to come out, "Momma, that's the best food I've ever had." We went back to the table and when I looked for my new-found favorite food, it was gone. I still don't know who ate it, but I exploded this time.

I became a foodie that day. I made up my mind right then and there that I would spend the rest of my life involved in the art of making people happy through serving them delicious stuff to eat. I didn't play with my cousins much during their holiday visits, I watched the elders cook, and even got to help some. I am in love with cooking and will never fall out of love with it, because it isn't the food that matters as much as it is the people. Nana taught me that. When I prepare a meal and finish with one of my family dessert recipes, and see how happy it makes those I served it to, confetti and balloons start going off in my mind. I could die right then and be ok with it, because my life has been fulfilled.

I have traveled all across this country and have lived in 5 different states. I have never met people who are happier than people from the South. I also have never met as many people in one area who are overweight. I don't believe that there is any correlation between the two; I think that the common denominator is the Southerners' love for sugar. After all, this is where sugar cane is grown, and sorghum syrup and molasses were created.

Desserts are more than just part of a meal; they are part of an entire cuisine. Southern food can be summed up in Pecan and Sweet Potato Pie, because a large percentage of the entrée's and side dishes didn't actually come from here, most were brought on ships and we adopted the ingredients and methods of cooking.

Daddy used to say that dessert was only for children because they were too young for alcohol after a meal. He said all sorts of things though, like "rainy days are only good for making tricycle motors" - Whatever that means. I prefer to hybridize his philosophy on dessert in a lot of cases and, as a tip of the hat to Uncle Buddy, I incorporate alcohol into dessert. And sometimes that liquor doesn't come from the store either, but from a friend of a friend's third cousin, twice removed, who lives up in the hills and knows an awful lot about working with copper.

But rum, flavored vodka, schnapps, coffee liquors, and in rare cases, bourbon, take some desserts to a whole new level. Already great for an aperitif, most are close by anyway. Baw Baw would disapprove, and Momma hates rum sauce in her Bread Pudding, but I think that it adds complexity and layers of exquisite flavor. Peach schnapps tastes more like a peach than a peach bought at most big-name grocery stores, so if that's all you can get, then add a tablespoon, or two, or three.

The Cardinal sins to me are the substitutes that the health "experts" tell us are going to save our lives. I will not use applesauce in the place of butter when baking a cake, nor do I condone that type of behavior. But strangely, it does work. First they told us to cut back on the fatty foods, now they tell us to eat more of them. All of the flip-flopping makes my head hurt, and it distracts me while I'm trying to get the butter, sugar, and heavy cream to form a perfect caramel sauce without breaking. These ingredients are your friends in cooking. Your real friends are counting on you to not serve them a boring, low-cal ending to their meal. Be their hero. Tell them a story. Just make sure that you do it "Southern Style."

All Butter Pie Dough

1 stick unsalted butter

1 ¼ cup all-purpose flour, plus more for dusting

½ tsp salt

1 tsp sugar

1 Tbsp buttermilk

3-4 Tbsp ice water, plus more if needed

Cut butter into small cubes and chill for 30 minutes.

Combine flour, salt, and sugar in a food processor and pulse a few times. Add butter and pulse until mixture resembles coarse sand.

Add 1 Tbsp of buttermilk and 3 Tbsp of ice water and pulse until dough starts to come together. Squeeze a little bit into a ball to see if it sticks together. If dough is too dry it will not stick and may need another Tbsp of ice water. If you get the dough too wet you can fix this by adding more flour, ½ Tbsp at a time.

Place dough on a floured surface and form into a disk shape. Wrap with plastic wrap and chill for at least 1 hour before rolling.

Remove chilled dough and place on a floured surface. Dust a rolling pin with flour and roll into a 10-11 inch circle. Fold dough in half so it is easy to handle and place in a pie dish. Trim extra crust around edges. Cover and place in refrigerator while you prepare filling.

*You can double this recipe if needed. Any extra dough can also be frozen for 2-3 months if wrapped in plastic.

German Chocolate Cake with Coconut Pecan Frosting

1 pkg. Baker's German Chocolate

½ cup boiling water

1 cup butter

2 cups sugar

4 eggs, whites and yolks divided

1 tsp vanilla extract

½ tsp salt

1 tsp baking soda

2 ½ cups cake flour, sifted then measured again

1 cup buttermilk

Melt chocolate in ½ cup of boiling water, then let cool. Cream butter and sugar until light and fluffy. Add egg yolks, one at a time, and beat well after each one is added. Add the melted chocolate and vanilla. Mix well. Sift together salt, soda, and flour, then add buttermilk and mix well. Add this mixture to chocolate mixture and beat at low speed in a standup mixer, or by hand, until batter is smooth. Beat egg whites until stiff, and then fold into batter. Pour into three lightly greased 9 inch cake pans. Bake at 350°F for 35-40 minutes. When done, let cool in pans before trying to remove.

For Coconut Pecan Frosting:

1 cup evaporated milk

1 cup sugar

3 egg yolks

1 ½ sticks butter

1 tsp vanilla extract

1 1/3 cups shredded coconut

1 cup pecans

Combine evaporated milk, egg yolks, butter, and vanilla in a saucepan. Cook over medium heat, stirring constantly, until mixture thickens, about 12 minutes. Remove from heat and add coconut and pecans. Beat until frosting is cool and thick enough to spread.

Spread frosting on the top of each cake and stack them three-high. Apply any remaining frosting to the top of the cake and let stand for 30 minutes before slicing.

Sweet Potato Pie

4-5 large sweet potatoes

1 stick unsalted butter

1 (14oz) can sweetened condensed milk

3 Tbsp all-purpose flour

½ cup sugar

½ cup brown sugar

2 large eggs

1 Tbsp vanilla extract

½ tsp ground cinnamon

¾ tsp ground nutmeg

2 (9 inch) pie shells, unbaked

Bake sweet potatoes in a 350°F oven for 1 hour. Let cool and peel. Mash potatoes in a large bowl until all lumps are removed. Reserve 3 cups.

In a separate bowl, mix butter, flour, condensed milk, eggs, sugars, vanilla extract, cinnamon, and nutmeg. Mix well then add to potatoes. Mix all ingredients well then pour into pie shells. Bake for 1 hour at 350°F on the middle rack of the oven. Remove pie from oven and let cool for 2 hours before slicing.

Blackberry Cobbler

5 cups fresh blackberries

½ cup water

1 ½ cups sugar, plus 1 cup for batter

1 ½ cups self-rising flour

1 cup whole milk

2 sticks unsalted butter

Combine blackberries, ½ cup water, 1 ½ cups sugar, and ¾ stick of butter in a pot and cook over low-medium heat for 25-30 minutes, mashing berries as they cook. When berries are cooked down and their juices have been released, set aside. Melt ½ stick of butter in a 12 inch cast-iron skillet and pour berry mixture directly in. Place in oven at 350°F while you prepare batter.

In a bowl, combine flour, milk, and 1 cup sugar, and mix well. When berry mixture is bubbling hot, remove from oven and spoon batter over the top, making odd-shaped biscuits all around the pan. Be sure to get plenty around the edges, because that's the best part. Dot top with remaining butter and return skillet to oven. Bake for 30-40 minutes, or until batter is golden-brown and crispy around the edges.

Cracker Cake

32 saltine crackers, rolled fine

2 cups sugar

2 cups chopped pecans

6 egg whites

1 tsp cream of tartar

1 ½ tsp baking powder

1 tsp vanilla extract

¾ cup shredded coconut

1 (8oz) can crushed pineapple, drained

2 ½ cups Cool Whip

Combine crackers, pecans, 1 cup sugar, and baking powder in a mixing bowl. Set aside.

Beat egg whites until stiff, then add 1 cup sugar and cream of tartar. Mix well.

Fold dry ingredients and vanilla extract into egg mixture and mix well. Pour into a greased 9x13 pan and bake at 350°F for 25 minutes, or until golden brown.

Cool and place in refrigerator for at least 2 hours. On chilled cake, spread Cool Whip, then sprinkle pineapple and coconut over top.

Double Berry Bread Pudding with White Chocolate Sauce

1 lb day old French bread, cubed

10 cups whole milk, divided in half in separate bowls

6 eggs

2 cups sugar

1 ½ sticks unsalted melted butter, plus 3-4 Tbsp for greasing dish

1 Tbsp vanilla extract

1 tsp cinnamon

1 tsp nutmeg

½ tsp mace

½ tsp salt

1 cup blueberries

1 cup blackberries

For White Chocolate Sauce:

¾ cup heavy cream

¾ cup white chocolate chips

2 tsp vanilla extract

1 stick unsalted butter

¼ cup light brown sugar

In a large bowl, soak bread and berries in 5 cups whole milk.

In a separate mixing bowl, beat butter and 2 cups sugar on low speed. Add eggs, one at a time, until all 6 are combined, then add 1 Tbsp vanilla extract, cinnamon, nutmeg, and remaining 5 cups of milk. Add this mixture to soaked bread and berries, then fold together with a spatula.

Preheat oven to 300°F. Using remaining butter, grease a 9x13 casserole dish. Pour mixture into buttered dish and bake for 75 minutes. Insert a toothpick into center; if the toothpick comes out clean, the bread pudding is done. If not clean, cook for another 10-15 minutes.

In a medium saucepan over low heat, melt butter and sugar together until sugar has dissolved. Add 1 cup white chocolate chips and melt, stirring frequently.

Slowly stir in all of the cream and combine well, then add vanilla and raise heat to medium. Stir constantly until sauce thickens and just starts to simmer around the edges, then remove from heat.

Serve bread pudding with sauce poured over the top.

Lindsey Gail's Bundt Cake

12 egg yolks

3 cups all-purpose flour, sifted then measured again

2 ½ tsp baking powder

½ tsp salt

2 cups sugar

1 tsp vanilla extract

1 cup cold whole milk

Preheat oven to 350°F and grease Bundt pan.

Beat egg yolks thoroughly. Whisk flour, baking powder, and salt together. Whisk sugar into egg yolks, a little at a time, then add vanilla and combine with flour mixture. Pour in milk and mix well.

Pour cake mixture into pan and bake for 50-55 minutes. Let cool for 30 minutes.

Katy Richard's Cream Cheese Blueberry Pound Cake

3 sticks unsalted butter

8oz cream cheese

2 cups sugar

3 cups all-purpose flour, sifted then measured again

1 ½ cups fresh blueberries

6 eggs

1 Tbsp vanilla extract

¼ tsp baking soda

1 tsp salt

For Lemon Glaze:

2 Tbsp melted butter

3 Tbsp milk

3 Tbsp lemon juice

2 cups powdered sugar

Zest of 1 lemon

Beat butter and cream cheese in mixer until smooth. Add sugar and beat until fluffy. Add eggs, one at a time, and then vanilla.

In a separate bowl, sift flour, salt, and baking soda, and then add to liquid mixture. Beat for 2 minutes.

Toss blueberries in a mixing bowl with flour to coat. Stir into cake mixture. Coat a standard bread pan with Bakers Joy spray (it will stick if you use anything else). Coat pan with sugar by sprinkling all inside the pan, then shaking out excess. Pour batter in and pat down with a spatula. Place pan in a cold oven, set the oven to 300°F, and bake for 90 minutes.

Cool 5 minutes and flip onto cooling rack. Let cake cool for 30 minutes, and then stand upright on a cake stand.

Combine melted butter, milk, lemon juice, and powdered sugar in a cold bowl. Mix until all lumps are gone and glaze is thin and smooth. Drizzle over top of cake. Sprinkle lemon zest over glaze and let cake stand for 20 minutes before slicing.

Coconut Pie

½ cup unsalted butter

½ cup sugar

¾ cup white Karo syrup

2 Tbsp honey

3 large eggs, lightly beaten

1 tsp lemon juice

½ tsp salt

1 ½ cups shredded coconut

1 (10 inch) unbaked pie shell

Preheat oven to 350°F. Cream butter well. Add sugar slowly, creaming until light and fluffy. Slowly stir in Karo, honey, eggs, lemon juice, and coconut. Pour into pie shell and bake for 55 minutes.

Key Lime Pie

Crust:

1 ½ cups finely crushed graham cracker crumbs

¼ cup brown sugar

4 Tbsp melted butter

Filling:

2 (14oz) cans sweetened condensed milk

½ cup sour cream

¾ cup key lime juice

2 egg yolks

1 Tbsp lime zest

Topping:

1 cup cold heavy cream

2 Tbsp powdered sugar

1 tsp lime zest

  In a medium bowl, combine all ingredients for crust and mix well with a fork. Pour mixture into a 9 inch pie dish. Using your fingers, press the crumbs firmly into the bottom and up the sides of dish. With the bottom of a cup flatten out crust to just under ¼ inch thick and trim sides evenly. Bake at 350°F for 10 minutes, until slightly browned. Allow crust to cool completely.

In a mixing bowl, whisk egg yolks and 1 Tbsp of lime zest together. Add condensed milk, lime juice, and sour cream and whisk thoroughly.

Scrape filling into your prepared pie crust and bake at 350°F for 15-20 minutes, until filling only wiggles slightly in the center. Let stand for 30 minutes, then place in refrigerator for at least 3 hours, but overnight is best.

In the bowl of a standup mixer with a whisk attachment, beat the heavy cream until soft peaks form. Add the powdered sugar and beat until medium peaks form.

Top the pie with the whipped cream and sprinkle 1 tsp of lime zest over the top. Return pie to refrigerator for at least 45 minutes before slicing. Serve cold.

www.ingramcontent.com/pod-product-compliance
Lightning Source LLC
LaVergne TN
LVHW020132080526
838202LV00047B/3925